QUEEN OF THE WITCHES

Jessica Berens

Hutchinson
LONDON

To Jessamy

© Jessica Berens 1993

The right of Jessica Berens to be identified as Author of this work
has been asserted by Jessica Berens in accordance with the Copyright,
Designs and Patents Act, 1988

This edition first published in 1993 by
Hutchinson

Random House UK Limited
20 Vauxhall Bridge Road, London SW1V 2SA

Random House Australia (Pty) Ltd
20 Alfred Street, Milsons Point, Sydney, NSW 2061, Australia

Random House New Zealand Ltd
18 Poland Rd, Glenfield, Auckland 10, New Zealand

Random House South Africa (Pty) Ltd
PO Box 337, Bergvlei, 2012, South Africa

A CIP catalogue record for this book is available from the British Library

ISBN 0 09 177553 1

Set in 10.5/12 ITC New Baskerville by
Pure Tech Corporation, Pondicherry, India
Printed and bound in Great Britain by
Mackays of Chatham PLC, Chatham, Kent

All the characters in this novel are entirely fictional

QUEEN OF THE WITCHES

THE COVEN OF COVENS

ANGERBODA
(Queen of the Witches)

Rythanwy	The Daughters of Branwen (Cardiff)	**Merlin**	The Grail Messengers (West London)
Themis	Handmaidens of Hermés (Carlisle)	**Bridget**	The Oracle of Queen Maeve (Northern Ireland)
Eumonia	The Daughters of Calatin (South London)	**Eirene**	The House of Phoebe (Cambridge)
Belladonna	The Faeries (Folkstone)	**Nepthys**	The Norns (East London)
Levanah	The Dark Women of Knowledge (North London)	**Vesta**	Sheila na Gigs (Sheffield)
Dana	The Sisters of Morrighan (Eire)	**Charles**	Thor's Hammer (Scotland)

CHAPTER ONE

Sheenah, High Priestess of the Divine Order of Isis and Director of the Witches' Liberation League, awoke on the morning of 2 February with a feeling of foreboding and gloom. Most of us, of course, suffer these emotions with monotonous regularity but are not advantaged by information pertaining to their sources. Sheenah, however, was lucky. She knew that Mars was responsible. Mars and Saturn, to be exact, which today were in opposition. An aspect similar to this had caused Pompeii to disappear. It boded natural disaster and was particularly depredatory to unfortunates like herself who, born with Jupiter in Aries, were preternaturally accident prone. Merlin the Magus, her friend from the Grimoire Bookshop in Soho, had even taken the trouble to leave a comforting message on her answering service. 'In the name of Hecate,' it said, 'thank the Goddess you're not ski-ing or something.'

She wondered whether she should stay in bed but feared that celestial malevolence would cause her to fall out and split her head open. Anyway, she could not stay in bed. Aspects or no aspects, there was much to do.

Today, the Festival of Imbolc and the celebration of the Fire Goddess Bridget, also marked the beginning of Witchcraft 1, a series of evening classes which she taught every year in the hope they would encourage people to become witches. There was an altar to be prepared, traditional Sabbat cakes to be baked, crystals to be annointed and aspectarians to be found.

So Sheenah, High Priestess of the Divine Order of Isis and Director of the Witches' Liberation League, bravely rose to face the day. She padded carefully across her bedroom and plucked a long green and gold caftan from her wardrobe.

1

Then, after ensuring that the legs of her chair were secure, she sat down in front of her dressing-table mirror and applied a generous layer of viridescent make-up to both eyelids. She did this with the automatic gestures born of familiarity for, with the help of a spongette on a stick, she had worn Frosty Shimmer of the Meadows for many years. This morning, however, in keeping with the combustive planetary atmosphere, her ocular region suddenly rose up in a fierce allergic reaction and, as tears rolled from itching eyes, her features homogenised into a crimson sheen.

Blindly she flicked through her herbal healing almanac and found a recipe based on the information that meadowsweet was anti-inflammatory and goldenseal would hasten the healing process. Searching through her supplies she located the recommended substances and made a cold compress. As she patted the cooling medicine on to her eyes, she caught sight of herself in the mirror and sighed. For here was a crone indeed. A crone of fifty-six speeding headlong through the last third of her life. Maiden and Matriarch she had been, and now, as Wiccan lore dictated for those who had experienced menopause, she was Crone. She sighed again. The bounty of wisdom and the calmness of inner peace were supposed to be the spiritual rewards of maturity, but today she felt as though she was Shakespeare's Weird Sister, the hell-hag of popular imagery.

Gloomy and lachrymose she descended to the kitchen to find that Catty was coughing in an alarming manner. Sheenah eyed the animal with distaste. 'I suppose you'll have to go to the vet,' she said.

The truth was that relations between witch and familiar were not all they could have been. Sheenah did not really like cats and only owned one because she felt that, as a witch and with a certain position to uphold in occult circles, she was obliged to have one.

Catty had been a gift from a farmer. She was the only survivor of a litter that had died from a mixture of smallness and inbred ill-health. Nervous that the kitten would not thrive, Sheenah had prayed to the cat goddess Bast and performed several powerful spells to ensure the pet's health and safety. Catty, as a result, had grown at a voracious rate, until

2

by the age of one she was the size of a small table. Her legs were thick, hirsute and caramel-coloured; her tail could break an arm with one blow, and her huge jaws seemed designed for the mastication of sides of beef.

She had been christened Catty for good reason. With this bulk came a pathology whose finer points are described in the true crime sections of bookshops. Amongst her multitudinous personality disorders was the habit of leaping into the air and attaching herself to the shoulders of unsuspecting visitors. The victims would then bend over like croquet hoops and scream in agony as four secateur-like claws dug into their flesh.

Recently Sheenah had been forced to confine Catty to the house because the neighbour's baby had reached the age when it wanted to pat things. Babies patted Catty at their peril. Sheenah, who lived in fear of a lethal contretemps, attempted to level out the animal's savagery with the aid of Lithium posited secretly into her food, but imprisonment and chemical dependency had done little to make Catty's character any more endearing.

If the stentorian wheezing of Catty had not been enough to undermine the enjoyment of her toast and 'natural' honey, Sheenah then turned on Breakfast Television to be greeted with the unwelcome sight of her arch enemy and nemesis, Myra, Clan Mistress and Wiccan Mother of the South London Sisters of Diana. Myra, all coiffured raven hair and jewellery that twinkled under the studio lights, was being interviewed about a 200-year-old oak tree on Clapham Common which was destined to be replaced by some public conveniences. The Sisters of Diana, it seemed, had taken the plight of the tree personally. One had chained herself to it and the rest were campaigning to raise public consciousness in order to pressurise the council to change its plan. The interviewer nodded sycophantically as Myra regaled her with details of the local authority's murderous attitude to South London's eco-balance.

'Huh,' Sheenah muttered to herself. 'The oak is nearly as old as she is.'

She entertained an attractive inner vision of cutting Myra in half with an athame and counting her rings until another hysterical cough from Catty brought her back to earth with a shudder.

'I neutralise that thought,' she said out loud, for, as any witch knows, the power of thought is great; entertain wicked notions and they will return to you threefold. It is the law of the Goddess.

Myra, Clan Mistress and Wiccan Mother, was, in fact, only fifty-one, five years younger than Sheenah. Younger, it has to be said, and more beautiful – dark, soignée and green-eyed against Sheenah's more endomorphic qualities. Sheenah did not resent women more physically perfect than her just because they were, but Myra had been responsible for the break-up of her marriage and one did not forget these things.

Some, she had to admit, might ask why anyone would want to run away with Harold.

Harold was a small man with a bald head, soft white physique and smooth feminine hands. The braver members of her coven still suggested that she had chosen him on the same principal that she bought her cars, which were always rusty and ignominious to lower the risk of them being stolen. But Sheenah knew that Harold's infinite subtleties of nature became apparent to those who patiently investigated. He was complicated. His emotions were intense, his soul was restless, and he became more intriguing as one drew closer.

They had lived in Battersea where Sheenah ran the Order of Hecate and where Harold worked as a hypnotherapist. She had often tried to persuade him to join the coven. Male energy was, after all, an essential component of working magic. But he had always refused. He said he needed his energies to help people stop smoking.

As an initiated High Priestess and leader of the Order of Hecate (which she had founded), Sheenah taught her members everything she knew – and those members included Myra, whom she had met on a CND march. Myra had been a talented adept. Psychic, intelligent, a natural healer, she could perform many types of divination (Tarot, Astrology, cartouche) and she was miraculous with arthritis and rheumatism.

But Myra's sun was in Scorpio, and Aries and Scorpios are doomed to defer, especially in a coven where balances are delicate and interpersonal relationships intense.

4

Tensions began over the ideological differences inherent in the practice of witchcraft. Sheenah, a traditionalist, adhered to the principles of the Old Religion and believed in the ancient rituals that had been handed down through generations of countryside nature worshippers. Furthermore she had been initiated when the rites of Wicca were illegal and 'skyclad' or naked ceremonies were avoided as being unnecessarily risky.

She did not believe that it was necessary to take one's clothes off in order to worship the Goddess. Myra, on the other hand, had been initiated by an Alexandrian. She was an enthusiastic nudist and caused dissension and controversy within the Order of Hecate by attempting to introduce nakedness to the esbats. Irreverent about the ancient symbology, she liked to improvise, modernise, write her own spells and charges and adapt the religion in ways that suited her and which, in Sheenah's view, were often ill-considered and without long-term benefit.

Then, before anyone could say 'Blessed be', Myra was calling herself a 'Psychic Counsellor', putting letters in front of her name, advertising in the classified section of *Wicca Weekly*, charging enormous fees and driving about in a chauffeur-driven Bentley. Sheenah felt this gave the Craft a bad name, a thing it did not need after hundreds of years of public opprobrium.

The press had caught on and Myra, photogenic and articulate, soon became an acknowledged spokeswoman. Every time there was a satanic murder her advice was sought, every Halloween she appeared to announce that, no, real witches did not fly about on broomsticks. This was an obsolete image that derived from an ancient fertility ritual. Soon she was fielding calls ranging from those who had lost their spaniels to those who thought they were possessed.

Sheenah had never overtly opined that as the head of the coven and the person with the most experience she should have been the one called forth to expound the ancient knowledge, for she had been aware that prideful resentment was both undignified and unsuitable for one attempting to follow the right-hand path.

Then she had made the mistake of introducing Myra to her Harold.

Odd, she thought; it had been Imbolc. Twenty-five years ago today.

She remembered the scene with crystalline clarity. They had met Harold in the Cock and Bottle pub after celebrating the Sabbat. There was Myra, wearing a tight, low-cut black robe, with a glass of tomato juice sitting like blood in front of her. Harold with his Guinness. And Sheenah (also in black but cut to a more generous empire line) unhappily fighting the finely tuned intuition that told her that Myra intended to seduce Harold for no reason other than the fact that he was there.

Soon after this Sheenah had suffered a series of debilitating stomach cramps and was admitted to hospital for tests. Ganglia of wires had been attached to various parts of her body, processions of medical students had prodded her and she had wondered if she was going to live. Then a friend told her that in her absence Myra had appointed herself leader of the Order of Hecate and was widely believed to be introducing Harold to sex magick.

As the doctors argued over possible prognoses for her mystery illness, Sheenah became certain that her condition was the result of astral attacks by Myra. The woman was unrestrained by fear of karmic consequences and she wanted Sheenah out of the way. Her prophecies were fulfilled the day that Harold appeared in the ward. Apologising profusely, he announced his intention to move out.

Two hours later, Sheenah's cramps disappeared as suddenly and inexplicably as they had appeared.

She had moved west where she could be sure she would not accidentally meet her ex-husband or his lover and bought a house with four floors and a small garden. The basement became a temple and she transformed the first floor (which had a bay window) into a shop selling magical swords, herbs, beeswax candles and the other commodities required for spell-making which at that time were difficult to find. She managed to make money from her readings (she used a crystal ball) and soon a new coven gathered around her. She never heard from Harold again.

6

Myra, however, was often talked about, both because she ran an astrological column in the *News of the World* and because she was sometimes on television. So it wasn't long before the news arrived that Harold had disappeared, leaving Myra with a small son.

Sheenah flicked the television switch to 'off'. The combination of campaigning Myra and coughing Catty was not life-enhancing. Anyway, the swelling on her eyes had receded slightly and she felt ready to tackle the cleaning of the temple.

Many witches painted their temples black, but Sheenah felt this was frightening and melodramatic. So the door of the sanctum was gold and bore a mural depicting the Goddess Isis who, although complete with the throne, uraeus and bracelets that were the traditional components of her ensemble, also seemed somewhat fatter and more relaxed than the representations seen on Egyptian sarcophagi. Indeed, the acute would observe that she looked suspiciously like Sheenah. Underneath her feet, in hieroglyphic-style typography, were the words, 'peace,' and 'blessed be'.

The room itself, which was large, had been decorated with textured purple and gold wallpaper teamed with purple velvet curtains. On the floor was the grey wall-to-wall carpeting that had been 'thrown in' with the price of the house. Around the edge were cumbersome second-hand sofas, whose insides occasionally sprang up and into the bodies of sedentary guests.

There was a Victorian fireplace in whose grate stood the display of pine cones and heather that Sheenah had collected on one of her Dormobile holidays to visit the Gardnerian witches in the New Forest. Above this the mantelpiece offered ornate candle holders with elaborate bases in the shape of gnarled claws, and photographs of various members of the Divine Order of Isis. Portrayed at hand-fastings, ceremonies of consecration and other pagan rituals, they were resplendent in their ceremonial dress.

In one corner, on a blackboard ready for Witchcraft 1, she had chalked the circle showing the Witches' Wheel of the Year. Divided into the eight Sabbats, North was the Winter Solstice and South the Summer Solstice.

7

On shelves constructed by Merlin the Magus (in return for a money-making spell) were her magickal collections of at-hames and knives, bottles of dried herbs for healing, Egyptian statuettes, incense burners, crystal balls from all over the world and, in pride of place on a red cushion with gold embroidery, her wand, a beautiful and ancient carved staff that Morgana, Mother of all the Witches in New England, had given her. Sheenah tended to save it for special occasions when evening wear was required and she had an audience. She used her less heavy, more practical hazel twig for every-day magic.

The bottom shelf was reserved for ongoing spells. Photo-gaphs of runaway children which she had charged with the power of Pluto (to aid intuitive revelation), curling news cuttings about Myra along with some St John's wort plucked at the time of the waning moon in an attempt to banish the evil she believed Myra was attempting to perpetrate against her. Sometimes she wondered whether the St John's wort had had anything to do with the disappearance of Harold from the life of Myra. She hoped that the Goddess understood she did not wish to interfere with the natural forces of the Web of Wyrd but merely to neutralise psychic molestation.

In the centre of the room was her altar, constructed from a card table with the material left over from the curtains thrown over it. On it, pointing north – the regime of the Archangel Uriel and the direction of mystery – was her silver goblet, a black candle, and the fissured fossil (representing earth) that she had found when she visited Wookie Hole in the Dormobile. To the east – the direction of air – there was a yellow candle (for communication) and some sea salt (for protection); and to the south – associated with the element of fire – was her antique censer and a little statuette of the Archangel Michael that she had bought for £2.50 from a Sikh in Shepherd's Bush Market. And, finally, west – the watery domain of Gabriel – stood her silver chalice. In the middle lay a pentacle, a cauldron and a statue of Isis surrounded by quartz crystals to enhance her energy.

Many modern witches thought of the Goddess as a crude feminist, a Cybele whose purpose was to compensate for cen-turies of rule by bearded and aggressive sileni. For Sheenah, though, the Goddess was the shining Egyptian woman who appeared in the visions of her childhood. Bathed in light she exuded a serenity very different to the pained figurines in the Catholic church frequented by Sheenah's mother. Unburdened by the agonies of martyrdom, Sheenah's Goddess represented the honourable qualities of womanhood. A patient friend, an empathetic healer, her impartial advice was the fruit of wisdom based on the experience of eternity.

It was in deference to this deity that Sheenah knelt in front of the altar. Then she lit a candle, threw some vervain over the flame (to empower herself for the following year) and prayed for the success of her evening class and the knowledge to know what was right for her pupils.

Then she hoovered the wall-to-wall carpet, dusted the altar and unmethodically wiped things with a damp cloth until, slightly bored, she went out to replenish the bird table with bread.

Sheenah's bird table, like most things in Sheenah's life, was imbued with mystical qualities. She was fairly sure that the vast robin who seemed to dominate bird-table social activity had been sent by her grandmother, both because of its florid hue (Granny Maldwyn had suffered from hypertension towards the end of her life) and because it had appeared on the tenth anniversary, to the hour, of her death.

The bird table was another reason why Catty was confined to the house.

Thinking of Catty reminded Sheenah that she had better take the animal to the vet. She groaned inwardly. Taking Catty anywhere was a complicated and gruelling procedure. She was so big that the only way her leviathan physique could be transported was strapped into an old children's pram. Catty resented this vehicle, so Machiavellian methods had to be devised to deceive her into supplication. Tricking Catty provided a strenuous intellectual challenge for – as Sheenah sometimes admitted after a glass or two of lager – there was the distinct possibility that Catty's IQ was a good deal higher than her own.

There was an icy wind blowing up and down the Shepherd's Bush streets and a grey vengefulness in the sky. Sheenah put her thermal underwear on beneath the caftan, pulled on her black cloak with the acrylic fur lining, placed lemon yellow ear-muffs over her ears and a pair of tortoise-shell Paloma Picasso dark glasses over her eyes, which were still slightly red. She did not want anyone at the surgery to think she had been crying or, more importantly, to see her without make-up.

'Come on, Catty darling,' she said encouragingly. The ferocious grimalkin growled and tried to spit but, undermined by the antipsychotic drugs that had been placed in her supper the night before, and by her mystery illness, she eventually allowed herself to be positioned in the Perambulette where she sat, back erect.

'I hope it doesn't rain,' Sheenah said in a futile attempt to ingratiate herself.

The deep-bellied, unwieldy Slumberspring Perambulette had been old-fashioned in the Fifties when Granny Maldwyn used it for transporting firewood. Now it was a collector's item. Designed for the slow parade of privileged babies in velvet collars around Kensington Gardens, its appearance in the street tended to attract attention from men who had businesses in the Portobello Road and were always on the look out for a bargain.

The weight of Catty, the heavy iron framework of the chassis and the fact that the wheels had rusted meant the Perambulette was almost impossible to propel.

'Glory be to the Goddess,' panted Sheenah. 'I'm sure it was never as heavy as this with the wood.'

She bent over, stretched out her arms and put her head down, as one does to push a car that has stalled in the middle of the dual carriageway. All that could be seen from behind was a headless black cloak, scarlet wool stockings and lace-up boots. This position also meant that she could not see where she was going so it was lucky that the vet's surgery was quite near. A ten-minute walk for a normal person with a lethargic goldfish, say, or ailing axolotl, but twenty minutes for an antique steered by a witch whose cardio-vascular system had never experienced anything more demanding than gardening.

She stopped for a rest at the organic fruit shop.

'Pity you lot can't do anything about the weather,' said the owner, whose eczema she had successfully cured a couple of months previously.

10

'Can't alter the laws of Mother Nature, Simon,' she answered, surveying the piles of misshapen fruit and malformed vegetation that constituted the shop's stock. 'How do you cook this then?' she said, pointing to a mottled ball whose box claimed it was from Ecuador.

'God knows,' said Simon.

'Pity you can't do anything about the weather,' said the Indian boy in the grocery-newsagent-video-hire emporium.

'Even we can't alter the laws of Mother Nature, Deepak,' she answered politely. 'Got the *Guardian*?'

'I don't know what you want to read that rubbish for,' said the boy looking up for a minute from his Sony Watchman.

'What do you read, then?'

'*Harper's and Queen.*'

'Cor, Mum, look at her,' said a child clutching a packet of Wotsits. 'She's got 'er cat in that pram.'

'Oh, come on, Shane.'

The surgery had a window looking out into the street and a placard announced the name of its resident practitioner – Mr Anwarbattishankar (B. Vet. Med MRCVS). A crowd of people and a malingering menagerie were already positioned on the plastic seats: children with rustling boxes full of unseen vermin, a girl with an overweight Lop rabbit and a punk rocker with a tapeworm wound around a stick.

'Hullo, Sheenah,' said a lady with chestnut hair and a white coat. 'Blessed be.'

'Hullo, Yvette,' said Sheenah. 'Blessed be.'

'Catty off-colour?'

'Yes. She's got a cough.'

'It's the time of the year. She needs a prayer to St Blaize.'

'I know. I thought of that. But Catty's not very spiritually inclined, as you know.'

Yvette did. The two women turned to look at the militant familiar who defied all seven Hermetic principles. She had placed herself in the only armchair in the waiting room. The Perambulette, too wide to fit through the door, was parked outside.

'Has she had a sedative?'

'Yes.'

'Thank goodness for that.'

The last time Mr Anwarbattishankar's surgery had been cursed with the presence of Catty, she had been mistaken for a lion cub by a myopic old lady with a pug. The pug, encouraged by its owner, became hysterical and Catty ran amok. Furniture had been broken and several people had been taken to St Charles' Hospital out-patients with minor injuries. Sheenah still received threatening letters from the lawyer of a man who claimed that his squid was still off its food as a result of this incident.

Some people in the waiting room might have been startled by Sheenah's appearance – the long, thick silver hair; the pink fingernails; the pentacles around the neck – and some might have considered her ostentatious. Yvette's senses, however, suffered no jolt. She had known Sheenah for years. Indeed, intent on watching Catty she might not have noticed what the High Priestess was wearing had it not been for the Paloma Picassos worn on a day devoid of sun.

'Something wrong with your eyes, Sheenah?'

'Allergy. Something to do with Mars and Saturn. They're in opposition. What can you expect?'

'Poor you. I've got a spell somewhere. Have you tried eyebright?'

'No. Goldenseal.'

'Perhaps you should try a hypoallergenic range.'

'Mr Anwarbattishankar appeared. 'Next,' he said.

'That's you,' observed Yvette. 'Good luck.'

Mr Anwarbattishankar, an Asian medic with neat, oiled black hair and spectacles with thick black rims, jumped back.

'Ah,' he said. 'Catty.'

'Yes,' said Sheenah. 'She's got a cough.'

'Has she been sedated?'

'Yes.'

'Thank goodness for that.'

After a brief examination Mr Anwarbattishankar, delighted to find that his hand was still attached to his arm, announced there was a slight infection at the back of Catty's throat. He gave Sheenah some antibiotics. Sheenah did not really believe in antibiotics but neither homeopathy nor the Bach Flower Remedies worked on Catty so she took the medicine and thanked him very much.

'Bye,' said Yvette. 'See you on Saturday.'

'Bye.'

When not assisting the vet, Yvette scried under the mystic name of Ursel. She was also secretary of the Witches' Liberation League which gathered on the first Saturday of every month. Meetings were held at members' houses and, this week, it was Yvette's turn to provide the finger buffet. Sheenah had introduced the idea of meals in an effort to discourage the interminable discussion that tended to greet the announcement of 'Any Other Business'. An effective psychological trick, it meant that League meetings, held in the tempting shadow of piles of chipolatas and the occasional crême brulée, adhered to subjects on the agenda and were not rendered boring or inefficient by solipsistic oratory.

Sheenah had launched the Witches' Liberation League when she moved to Shepherd's Bush in 1965. The Witchcraft Act had been replaced by the Fraudulent Mediums Act in 1951 and several illuminating books had consequently been written, but neither these nor the change of law precipitated any fundamental shift in public perception. Witches were the bogeywomen of the collective unconscious, at best mad and at worst ugly. Sheenah had always resented the popular portrayal of gurning harridans. There were no green polyps on her face, as far as she could see. Her teeth had been quite expensive and, despite the gardening, there was nothing hunched about her deportment.

There were many high priestesses, hierophants, psychopompi and second-degree initiates who wished to wear their pentacles and talk of their beliefs without being ostracised. Many feared that if they did so they would be dismissed from their jobs or that explosives would arrive through the post. Sheenah felt that witches should have the same right to worship, free from persecution, as any other religion in a democratic country. So the League began as an informal support group for those who wanted to 'come out'. It expanded under the pressure of Sheenah's determination. Her emotions had

13

been stirred by the perfunctory departure of her husband and, adrenalin stimulated, she applied herself to the campaign with the single-minded energy of one to whom the quest to raise public awareness had become a personal mission. This, combined with the fact that she was childless, and thus blessed with spare time, meant that the project benefited from persistence. The Witches' Liberation League managed to forge relationships with newspaper editors, politicians and policemen. By the end of the Sixties it was quite high profile. Members picketed the premiere of *Rosemary's Baby*, they lectured in schools and they provided legal advice to those who felt that their civil rights had been violated. They were in tune with the Zeitgeist (ecological awareness, feminism, quests for alternative deities) and by 1969 there were 25,000 names on the mailing list.

Witchcraft 1 was one of the results of these successes. Sheenah received hundreds of letters from people asking how they could join up and where she bought her clothes. Aware that she had burdened herself with a certain social responsibility (the craft of Aradia is impracticable for some, and in the wrong hands can actually be dangerous) but that there were advantages in increasing the fold (the more witches there were the less likely they were to be dismissed as spooky delinquents), she formulated a series of lectures that were designed to give the aspiring postulant a grounding in the history of witchcraft and the basics of magic.

Over the years she had attracted her fair share of lunatics – one ungifted acolyte had put on a pointed hat and robbed a bank – but in general Sheenah was quite proud of her graduates. Many were running powerful conservation groups, one was very high up in Warner Bros, there were several backbenchers and countless healers.

She advertised the course in *Wicca Weekly* and handed out flyers in occult bookshops. Merlin always took a dozen or so. He had also helped her write the advertisment.

IS THERE MAGIC IN YOUR LIFE?

Sheenah, High Priestess of the Divine Order of Isis and Director of the Witches' Liberation League, is one of England's best known witches. Every year Sheenah runs a course of evening classes for those who wish to know more about the Wiccan way. Astrology, magic, rituals, spells and the history of witchcraft are covered, and at the end, if the student is judged to be ready, he or she may graduate to Witchcraft 2 which prepares for initiation into a coven.

Witchcraft 1 starts on 2 February (the Sabbat of Imbolc) and ends on 1 May (Beltane). There are twelve sessions held on Wednesdays, the days of Mercury, from 7 pm to 9 pm. The fee, £50, covers talks given by visiting lecturers, refreshments and paper, but not the price of tools and magickal equipment which participants will be expected to provide for themselves.

Please write to the address below stating your name, age, star sign and reasons for wishing to take up the Craft.

DROP BY FOR A SPELL.

Blessed be.

Sheenah.

Sheenah thought that 'Drop by for a Spell' was going far too far, but Merlin, who fancied himself as a bard, insisted that jokes would make her image more alluring.

After the visit to the vet, Sheenah and Catty ate fish for their lunch and watched *Neighbours.* Then she sat down in the small study that served as her office. This was equipped with a computer which listed her regular clients' astrological details (essential as an aid to accurate divination), and spells which would not be dangerous if read or used by a novice. The powerful conjurations were locked in the safe. Sheenah knew little about computers and, having read about hacks and viruses, believed her diskettes were shockingly vulnerable to security violation.

The hardware was programmed by Yvette, who was both computer literate and familiar with the magic required to mend it when the screen went blank for no apparent reason. There was one month when it shut itself down so often that Sheenah thought a hex had manifested itself, but a man from the computer company told them it was static from the wall-to-wall carpeting.

She lit a sandalwood stick, to aid concentration, and chose a cassette tape by Tony Tantra and the Truth Vibrations.

15

Tony was, according to the label, 'a New Age musician whose compositions on the Uileann pipe are dedicated to opening the chakras of the mind'. Then she extricated a file and reread the letters she had received from those who wished to attend the course. These were requested not in order to pre-judge the applicants, but as a defence against involvement with serial killers. In the past she had received correspondence written in the sender's own blood, awful wax dolls with staring curranty eyes and photographs of Jim Jones. She knew that the creators of these would not be susceptible to spiritual enlightenment. The teachings of the Old Religion would be wasted on them. If SAEs were enclosed, she wrote back suggesting that the writers' money could be more profitably invested elsewhere.

Four people had applied to join Witchcraft 1. Not very many but she preferred to teach four serious students than a large class with a high drop-out rate.

Mmm, she thought. Two boys and two girls. Even balance of animae here.

One, on recycled paper, was from a woman called Melinda. 'I sell crystals and bongs in Camden,' she wrote. 'I am a Cancer and a vegan.'

The second, from an address in Eaton Terrace, had huge, looped handwriting that eddied about the paper like a balloon race. Rosaleen Arundell said she was Pisces and hoped she would get a place on the course although she was sure they were very full.

One of the men, Cuthbert Cuthbertson, was Sagittarius and had recently joined the police force in the hope of becoming a dog handler. 'I don't think,' he added, 'that my interest in the occult will get in the way of my work.' The last had been hand-delivered and was from a person who had enclosed a money order for £50 and a piece of paper on which, in black ink, the name 'Steve' had been signed.

CHAPTER TWO

As the cosmic disharmony of Mars and Saturn had caused disruption in the life of Sheenah, so too was it affecting the day of Rosaleen Arundell.

She had set the kitchen alight by leaving a wedge of toast under the grill while she stood in front of the bathroom mirror doing her 'I Love Myself' psycho-physical breathing exercises. Engrossed in sticking out her tongue, withdrawing it on the count of five and repeating the rote (recommended in the book *The Prana Way of Life*) 'I am beautiful, I am lovely', she had failed to notice the smell of burning Laura Ashley tiles.

Five fire engines parked in Eaton Terrace at 9.30 am provided an efficient obstacle to the flow of commuting traffic. The fireman observing from his position on top of the crane announced that the congestion stretched back to Victoria.

After the conflagration had been quenched and she had refreshed the brigade with digestive biscuits and glasses of Coca Cola, and after the street had cleared of honking cars and men in suits waving their fists in the direction of her house, she walked to Luigi's Patisserie in the King's Road to buy a number of cream cakes with which to calm her nerves.

Back at home she lay on the sofa eating custard *milles feuilles, amaretto* truffles and dairy slices and wished she had a boyfriend.

Jesus. She was twenty-three. If she didn't get one soon it would be too late.

Scenes from the disheartening debacle that was her love life floated across her cerebral screen.

Terence Grey, she had to admit, had been her fault. He was nearly forty and it had been discomfiting living with the fear

17

of his imminent death. No. The departure of Terence Grey had not caused unbearable emotional derangement. He was not the tragedy. Andrew Grateman was her tragedy.

Andrew Grateman was a playwright she had met at a party. He had impressed her by lowering himself through a skylight on a length of rope and offering her some Space Dust. Even with minute orange particles exploding in his mouth he was captivating. After dating for a couple of months she had fallen in love with him, and he had broken her heart by failing to reciprocate the range of complicated passions he had unintentionally stimulated. Commuting between his houses in London and California, he rarely returned her calls, and when he did it was to say that he was speaking from a car phone on the Strip, and did she have Sarah Stormont-Darling's telephone number as he had dropped his address book in the swimming pool at Gore Vidal's house?

She never cried in front of him but she had often hoped to die.

She still went to see his plays, despite the fact that one, at the Royal Court, had featured a scene in which a woman's head was removed with a tin opener. Andrew Grateman's creative vision, influenced by Jack London, Russ Meyer, Edward Bond and Samuel Beckett, presented itself in the form of titles like *Late Night Chopping*, *Mall Murderer* and *Pass the Meat, My Sweet*. Some had been made into successful films. Hollywood lucre had bought his pink mansion in Kensington, a pink mansion outside which Rosaleen often sat in her Peugeot 205 watching to see who was coming in and out.

Her friends tried to tell her that Andrew Grateman was a very unpleasant man whose plays were nearly as horrific as himself. Cheer up, they said, count your blessings. At least you're rich and look good on a horse. But Rosaleen was destined to be tortured.

Andrew Grateman and Terence Grey were not atypical members of Rosaleen's circle. The men of Rosaleen's circle tended to be keen on their dog, their horse, their gun and their mother, in that order. It was very difficult to force oneself up the priority list, particularly as the county matriarchy, aware of the circumstances of Rosaleen's background, had concluded that there was quite enough insanity in its families already.

The Arundell family had lived in Grimsby Hall, Gloucestershire, for many years and until recently had enjoyed a reputation for common sense and rectitude. They had managed to increase the fortune obtained by their ancestor 'Charles the Bore' (who had stolen it during campaigns on behalf of William of Orange) by investing with percipience during several agricultural depressions that could have been detrimental to the estate. They were neither profligate nor impetuous and they tended to marry wisely and well. So it had come as a crashing surprise to everybody when Charles Arundell (Rosaleen's father) announced his engagement to a woman he had met in the Green Man pub in Harrods. The rumour had circulated that Charles Arundell was mentally ill, and he had never quite managed to shake it off.

Rosaleen was not, as far as she could tell, mad, but she did suffer (according to Andrew Grateman) from a debilitating form of low self-esteem which warped her perspective. Andrew Grateman was very interested in the diverse neuroses caused by paranoia. Although he suffered from none himself, he enjoyed observing them in others in order to purloin the more maniacal computations for his work.

It had been the anguish caused by Andrew Grateman's cruelty that had lead indirectly to Rosaleen's decision to become a witch.

The day after he had stood her up in Le Caprice she went to the self-help section of W. H. Smith and bought an instruction manual on how to attract boys. Soon she became as addicted to survival guides as some people are to romantic novels, for, it could be argued, similar reasons.

She progressed quickly to personal growth books that told her it didn't matter if one was not blessed with a wide choice of admirers because it was more important to eradicate negative patterns, overcome old beliefs, take positive action, grow through pain, face up to fear and learn how to love oneself.

Greedily Rosaleen assimilated the philosophies and opinions offered by orientals who had eaten a lot of yoghurt, strident women from Connecticut who were proof of the

19

power of positive thought, and bearded messengers who could cure melanoma with their bare hands.

And so she learned of the mystical phenomena connected with menstruation (' "Love Your Blood" – a message from a discarnate entity'). She studied Yogi and Sufi, Kabashi and Kundalini. Sweeping through colonic irrigation, Candida and nuts she pored over the rejuvenating characteristics of betacarotene, germanium, selvite, niacin and bioflavonoids. And she filled out the questionnaire in the back of Mahatma Cote's classic, *The Development of the Brain by Bananas.*

Although she put very little of this advice into practice for more than four days, reading about how to feel better made her feel better. At least she was distracted. Meditating about the effects that certain fruits were supposed to have on the subconscious helped her to forget about Andrew Grateman and his Paul Smith shirts, Kelim rugs and smell of limes.

She had finished *The A-Z of Diverticulosis* and was looking for a book entitled *Charisma – Your Guide to Getting It* when she walked into the Grimoire Bookshop in Soho.

The exterior of the Grimoire Bookshop offered little clue as to its contents, consisting as it did of an unwashed window in which there was a depressed display of dried herbs and seaweed. It could have been anything from a Chinese super-market to a peep show.

Once inside, however, the owner's pride was apparent. The incense of jasmin wafted to the nostrils. In shadowy corners there were multi-coloured candles, glass jars full of bladderwrack, boxes of tarot cards, back copies of *Pagan Periodical,* silver pentacles, love spells in small gold packets and ornamental castles made out of Murano glass.

Behind a glass-fronted cabinet, in which rows of magic wands were displayed, sat a man wearing a black and gold tracksuit with 'Magick' written on it. His long white beard was partially hidden behind a copy of the book he was reading.

'Good morning,' he said. 'Good Christmas?'

'No,' replied Rosaleen. 'I hate Christmas.'

'Quite right,' said the man putting *The Cult of the Black Virgin* down on the counter and gazing at her with bright blue eyes. 'Frightful reminder of Constantine's oppression, I always say. Were you looking for anything in particular?'

Rosaleen didn't like to say a boyfriend so she said, 'Charisma.'

'The quality or the book?'

'Well, both really.'

'Oh dear. Bad as that, is it?'

Rosaleen suddenly felt irrational tears well up. Embarrassed she turned away and found herself looking straight into the eyeless mask of the god Pan. Taken by surprise, she screamed.

The purveyor of esoteric items descended from the high stool on which he had been perched, like St Simeon of Stylites, and noting that there was no ring upon Rosaleen's hand said:

'Boyfriend?'

'Ex-boyfriend.'

'Poor lovvie.' He reached behind her ear and produced an egg.

Rosaleen stared at him.

'I'm Merlin,' he said, offering a right hand on which the nails were smooth, manicured and a little long to be entirely conventional.

'Rosaleen Arundell.'

As she said this, Merlin scribbled her name on to a piece of paper, did some calculations on his fingers and said, 'Pisces?'

'Yes,' she said, amazed. 'How did you know?'

'Numerology, my dear. It can tell the wonders of the universe.'

'Really?'

'Yes. I'm Aquarius, by the way, like Neil Diamond, so we should be all right.' He looked again at the paper over which his eldritch sums were sprawled. 'Yes. There are too many fives, you see, and threes. It's a bad combination for poor old Pisces. Nice people, but tend to be so emotional. Ruled by their emotions, they are. They make very good librarians. You haven't considered that as a profession, have you?'

'I haven't really got a profession, unless you count helping in the Sue Ryder charity shop once a week.'

'No,' he said, fingers flying over a calculator. 'I can see money. Lucky you.' He flicked an invisible mote of dust from the surface of the counter. 'The thing is, Rosaleen,' he continued, 'I feel there is a lot of luck here, a lot of luck. The

21

good times are just around the corner, as it were, but you've got to take control, darling. The Goddess isn't out to get you, you know. There are cherries out there, all ripe and ready to be plucked.'

He produced a live dove from his sleeve.

'How did you do that?' said Rosaleen.

'Magic,' he said. 'Would you like a cup of my special Witches' Brew tea?'

'Yes, please. Who's the Goddess?'

'The Goddess,' said Merlin, pressing the button in of the electric kettle and removing one of the glass jars from its place on the shelf, 'is the Mother of All. The Triune Deity. The Great Giver. The Goddess is the Maiden, Mother and Crone. Hecate and Diana, Aradia and Venus. She is our Ruler.'

'Like God, only a woman?'

'You could say that.'

'Ah.'

'Yes, and if you believe in her you can believe in yourself, and if you believe in yourself, Rosaleen, you can do anything.'

Rosaleen had read this theory several times in her self-help books but she had never heard about the Mother of All before.

'I have tried to help myself,' she said, 'but it never seems to work.'

'That's because in here,' said Merlin, patting the back of his head with his palm, 'you're not convinced. Right in the bottom part of the brain that used to be a lizard, you're not convinced.'

'So what do I do?'

'Well,' he offered, pouring boiling water on to olive green leaves. 'You need magic.'

Then he told her about Sheenah. Witches, he believed, were genuine modernists because they were evolving a philosophy that was practicable and relevant to everyday life in the twentieth century. The celebration of the Divine Feminine Principle was the natural effect of patriarchy; concerns with peace and nature were inextricably connected with the survival of civilisation. Sheenah, he insisted, could change Rosaleen's life.

'And,' he flowed on, 'what is more, Sheenah will soon be Queen of the Witches.'

'What?' said Rosaleen, not because she hadn't heard but because she hoped he was going to clarify this point.

'Queen of the Witches, Queen of the Witches, Queen of the Witches,' he sang. 'It's the most important thing you can be if you're a witch. It's like the Pope. It's the highest honour you can receive.'

'Who decides who'll be Queen?'

'Good question, very good question indeed!' enthused the Magus, waving his arms about like somebody attempting to land a plane on an illegal runway in Bolivia. 'It's a tradition that goes back hundreds and hundreds of years. The Queen of the Witches is elected by the Coven of Covens.'

'What,' said Rosaleen, 'is that?'

She was aware that a whole new world was being revealed to her, a world whose mores functioned autonomously and unaffected by contemporary events.

'Oh, dear,' said Merlin, 'I shouldn't really be telling you this. It's supposed to be a secret.'

'Please go on.'

'Oh, all right. I just can't help it. It's so exciting. The Coven of Covens represents all the witches of the United Kingdom and Eire. It started during the Burning Times as a kind of network to help those who had been sentenced to death to escape and start new lives in different parts of the country.'

'Like the resistance?'

'Yes. Anyway, now it is more of an administrative body, organising events and esbats and meetings, deciding on policies if there is a press question and, in general, dedicated to preserving our welfare.'

'So you're one?'

'Yes, darling. I'm the secretary. There are thirteen members including the Queen. Each member represents an area. The nominees are put forward and then, at Lammas, August the second, the Queen of the Witches is elected. Mind you, there hasn't been a new Queen for ages because Angerboda keeps getting voted back in, but now she's sixty-five she wants to retire. It's very hard work, you see.'

23

'So what's in it for the Queen?'

'Apart from the prestige, you mean? Well, it's a very powerful position, very powerful indeed. You are the official spokesperson for the thousands of witches in England, Ireland, Scotland and Wales, you make an enormous amount of money on the American lecture circuit and you have access to the Coven of Coven's *Very Moste Secrete Booke of Witchery* which is supposed to reveal the most potent spells in the history of the world. It's a responsible office requiring someone with impeccable integrity – particularly as the Coven of Covens is very rich due to the fact that so many pagans bequeath it money when they die.'

'So doesn't everyone want to be Queen?'

'Oh, yes,' Merlin affirmed emphatically. 'There'll be other nominees, of course, but Sheenah's the favourite. She's popular, she's a hereditary witch and she's known for her work with the Liberation League.'

'What about you?' inquired Rosaleen, thinking he would probably like to be asked.

'Me, darling? I can't be Queen! Members of the Coven of Covens aren't eligible: theirs is a lifetime appointment, you see, and disqualifies them from going any further. The Queen has to be an outsider. I might have Saturn in Gemini but frankly, darling, I wouldn't want the responsibility.'

By the time she had finished her cup of Witches' Brew, which tasted like peppermint, Rosaleen was convinced about the power, mastery and wisdom of the leader of the Divine Order of Isis. She took the flyer Merlin handed her.

'You have to write a letter of application,' said Merlin. 'Not everybody is suitable. But I'll put a word in for you.'

'Thank you,' said Rosaleen.

CHAPTER THREE

Myra, Clan Mistress and Wiccan Mother of the South London
Sisters of Diana, having returned from her interview, was
watching a black and white drama on her Securivision television set. The screen, which recorded the picture picked up
by a video camera hidden above her front door, showed a
milkman. Crouched on all fours, he was shouting through
the letter box about the matter of a sum of £74.76 in unpaid
milk arrears.

'Madam!' he roared. 'This is the fifth time this has happened. Creamy Dairies are sick and tired of it. They are
threatening legal action. It's not as if you can't afford it, Gawd
knows.'

The milkman was not blind. Through the letter box he
could see a hallway lined with thick ecru carpet in which
there were William Kent giltwood piers glass mirrors and a
Louis XV marquetry and ormolu bureau. He knew little of
antiques, but his wife occasionally forced him to accompany
her to a superstore in Brent and furniture like this was not
available there.

He knew he was being listened to. He could feel it in his
bones, and he was aware that people would turn out their
lights and lie on their floors when they heard the whirr of his
float on bill days. The dishonesty of Joe (as he called the
public) never failed to amaze him and he said so frequently
in the Creamy Dairies canteen.

His exhortation ended with a loud chorus of threats and,
eventually, having pushed the offending account through the
letter box, he stomped down the lane, milk crate clinking like
a kindergarten percussion class, and climbed furiously into
his float.

'PALLAS ATHENE!' screeched Myra. 'WHAT IS THE MILK-MAN DOING COMING TO THE FRONT DOOR? WE HAVE A BACK DOOR I BELIEVE. SEVERAL BACK DOORS . . .'

Silence.

A line of moisture, appeared on Myra's pale upper lip. Her thin mouth pursed so that it disappeared, then, suddenly, it emitted a yell of shocking intensity.

The people who lived two houses down ran out of their gate thinking an animal had been run over in the road.

'WHERE IN THE HELL ARE YOU?'

Footsteps clattered from the back of the house wherein lay the kitchen.

'ATHENE!!!'

A teenage girl with large ears appeared. Her name was, in fact, Karen but Myra, who had plucked her from the card-board box in which she lived outside Peter Jones, had re-named her Athene after the Greek goddess of war. She hoped that the girl would, under tutelage, become a novice and act as her handmaiden during ceremonies – a position which required someone at the pubescent stage of life.

Pallas Athene wore a light blue uniform with a white cap and pinny.

'I'm sorry,' she squeaked.

'Don't cower,' said Myra.

Her tone was chill and cold and her green eyes bored into the nervous girl. 'It wouldn't take much for me to fire you.'

Pallas Athene thought of the cardboard box and the cold and the police and shivered involuntarily.

'Yes,' said Myra, apparently able to read her thoughts. 'So in the name of Beelze-bloody-Bub get my breakfast. Now!'

Pallas Athene ran.

Myra sat herself down on one of her beautiful Queen Anne spoonback walnut dining chairs and looked at the polished maple of the dining room table on which stood the procession of antique silver statuettes that were responsible for the complicated range of security devices.

Pallas Athene crept about pouring coffee out of an ornate silver pot, then from a Luxe-E-Warm Hostess Trolley she served her employer brains, kidneys and stewed tongue. Al-though in many ways this scene was an ordinary one, merely a tableau of a rich matron being served her breakfast, the presence of Myra endowed it with theatricality, for her appearance was dramatic. This was not only because she dyed her hair and eyebrows the shade seen on the heads of young women in Mediterranean countries, or that she had a widow's peak that emphasised the symmetry of her heart-shaped face. She was also very well dressed in the way that wealthy women sometimes are, a way that manages to advertise their fortune without actually declaring their net worth in symbols upon their chests. She inclined towards tailored suits in primary colours, gold jewellery and hand-made shoes with needle-sharp heels. Her feet were small and delicate, as, indeed, was she, but this escaped most people's observation because her presence was that of somebody taller. There was nothing of the minikin about Myra, nothing blurred or indistinct. She was commanding. The symbols of wardrobe and coiffure emphasised this fact but, in the end, they were only special effects. Myra's self-possesssion was fuelled from within.

'Okay, you can go,' Myra said to her servant. She wished to be left in peace so she could study her shares in the *Financial Times*. As the world of Heng Seng and All Ordinaries unfurled in front of her, her eyes darted up and down the Gilt-Edged and Electricals, the Unlisted Securities and Commodities.

One thing that can be said of sorcery, she thought to herself. It's a very good combination with money.

Myra's stocks were up. It seemed that Myra's stocks were always up. She bought an uncanny percipience and nerve of steel to the art of trading. Her broker often wondered about her sources of information and hoped to God that she wasn't involved in anything that could implicate him.

Myra did have access to inside information, but not of the kind that her broker imagined. For Myra had invoked the powers of the Archangel Choronzon to help her divine the arcane undulations of the stock market. The Prince of Darkness saw all and he, together with her knowledge of the Zodiac, had helped her make a fortune. Consequently her skills were revered from City desks in Docklands to boardrooms in Wall Street. Her magic was so effective it sometimes surprised even her. Never afraid to exert her will in order to

27

fulfil its ambition, most precepts were adjusted to suit her whims. Her white magic had easily turned grey and, after the successful seduction of Harold, proceeded quickly to black. She had been careful never to reveal this spiritual transmogrification. Even the South London Sisters of Diana laboured under the misapprehension that their High Priestess was a white witch dedicated to the power of good.

She put down the newspaper and picked up a copy of *Connoisseur* magazine. Flicking through, she made a mental note to have her William and Mary torchères valued, to find out how much it would cost to restore the Georgian dumb waiter she had seen in the Fulham Road, and to check the housekeeping accounts.

The telephone rang.

She hoped it was her broker.

It wasn't.

It was Sophia Loren.

'Sofeeaa!' she exclaimed with a warmth most people reserve for those who have just pulled them out of quicksand.

The supernova wished to be informed about the astrological aspects relating to a proposed offer to make a film with 'Hurricane' Harry, the legendary kick-boxer. She needed the money, she said, but 'Hurricane' was so bossy. She didn't know if she could bear to be on location with him for eight weeks in Death Valley.

'Let me check my charts, lovely. I'll ring you back, are you in Switzerland?'

'*Si.*'

Bloody Italians. They had no sense of timing. It wasn't even 9.30. But she rushed to her study and pulled the file marked 'Loren' out of the Sheraton desk.

'Typical bloody Virgo, neurotic workaholic.'

Consulting her ephemeris and atlas, and making allowances for sidereal times, she did some calculations then rang Sophia Loren's chalet in Luzerin and told her on no account to make a film with 'Hurricane'. Apart from the fact that he was cursed with an afflicted Saturn, no Virgo with any sense would commit themselves to long-term projects or money-making ventures until at least April when there was a new moon in Taurus.

'And just remember, darling,' Myra said darkly, 'he was born on the same date as Stalin.'

Then, checking up on her own planetary status, and noting the position of Mars and Saturn, she rang her broker and told him to sell her shares in Polly Peck.

'But they're up 320 per cent,' he argued.

'I don't care. Sell them.'

Then she called up a client who had just been head-hunted by Solomon Brothers and said yes, she would be delighted to accompany him to the Speculators and Investors annual ball.

Myra was enjoying the rewards of upward mobility. Her Grade II listed Georgian mansion had thirty rooms and a view over Clapham Common. Her Mistress of the Stars astrological column was syndicated in fourteen publications and, since she had predicted the crash of '74, she was paid generous consultancy fees by companies in Tokyo, New York and Hong Kong. Soon she was to star in her own television show which the BBC had scheduled in a prime-time slot.

And soon she would be Queen of the Witches.

Myra had coveted the position for many years. This was not only because her Scorpionic sun allowed her to appreciate the enervating effects of promotion, but because she knew that the pages of *The Very Moste Secrete Booke of Witchery* would grant access to secrets whose combined power was inestimable. The Grimoire was a legend. Its marvels were so incendiary that only the reigning Queen of the Witches was allowed to touch it and, as Guardian, it was also her responsibility to prevent others from reading it. She had to swear an oath (on a petrified Hand of Glory) that she would perform these tasks. Should she fail in them, she was doomed to suffer a curse of death by all four elements. Angerboda was said to be so nervous about the book that she kept it locked up in the Bank of England.

No one knew how old the *Booke of Witchery* was because experts were prevented access to ascertain its antiquity. But it was known that thousands of magicians, witches, Druids and alchemists had contributed their knowledge to its pages. It contained their spells, their incantations, their talismen and their offertories. Thus it was said that the *Booke of Witchery* contained the secret of the Cabala (as whispered to Moses by God); the unpublished prescriptions of Paracelsus and the truth about the power of the Sator square. The reader could learn how to raise the 72 demons of Solomon's *Lemegeton*; how to communicate with the guardians of the sefiroth and how to produce the Philosopher's Stone.

Myra realised that the hermetic wisdom in this volume, combined with the knowledge that was already hers, would enable her to achieve anything she wanted. Her options would become limitless.

She had been aware, thanks to her training in applied astro-psychology, that Angerboda's reign would be a long one, so she had empowered her ambition with secrecy and had not obstructed her aim by putting herself forward because she knew that even if she won a nomination, she would lose against Angerboda. Failure has an uncanny way of clingings to the loser and inspiring loss of confidence. To sustain the respect of the electorate, Myra had to triumph the first time. So, having waited until the firmaments were cosmologically correct, she had easily won the South London by-election. Now all she needed was the support of the majority in the Coven of Covens. With this in mind, she descended to the bottom of the house to consult the Angel of Death.

Myra's shrine to Satan was hidden behind the temple in which she led the innocent rituals of the Sisters of Diana. The Dark Arts were unpopular amongst the goody-goody activists of her sorority, and the practice of Black Magic disqualified one instantly and without redress from competing for the Queen of the Witches.

She drew the curtain behind the altar and entered a hidden passage in which there was a black chantry. It was cold because the walls were made of stone and there was no heating. It was dark except for the flicker of candlelight, and there was a feeling of being stared at by hundreds of pairs of malevolent eyes. The smell of damp mingled with that of faded myrrh. On one wall there was a painting of the Tibetan goddess Tara, wearing a tiger skin and a necklace of skulls, standing astride a smoking funeral pyre.

The altar, trapezoidal, was covered in black velvet. On it stood black candles, aspergillum, censer and assorted coffin nails. Here too was a picture of Baphomet, the Judas Goat, who represents the powers of darkness, and an inverted pentagram with the three points representing the trinity denied. Next to the Chalice of Ecstasy and a ceremonial sword lay the *Books of Belial* and *Leviathan* and her own *Book of Shadows* which outlined the more useful steps of Enochian law.

Myra removed her Hardy Amies suit and, naked, knelt down in the middle of the circle painted in front of the altar. Baphomet sneered down at her.

She closed her eyes in order to connect with the Furious Hordes and to create a mental state suitable for attracting daemons. The most important step was to relinquish guilt. This for Myra was easy, because guilt was an emotion of which she had had little experience. As she breathed deeply, the familiar sensation of invincibility came upon her.

'Oh, Choronzon,' she said, 'father of all the Brothers of Darkness, Initiator of Terror and Pain, grant me the magnificent privileges of the infernal gods so that my magic may be the most powerful of all.'

The flame on top of the black candle flickered a little and there was a breeze. She could hear the footsteps of the servants in the kitchen above and the grumble of the lorries around Clapham Common, but Choronzon, Conjurator of Torture and Madness, did not manifest himself as he sometimes did – a glowering and ghastly figure swathed in robes of opaque luminosity.

Myra tried again.

'Oh, Choronzon!' she cried. 'Great and Most Masterful, let me be Queen of the Witches and I will do anything.'

CHAPTER FOUR

Angerboda lived in a cottage in Somerset. She and her two granddaughters, Frigga and Freya, were enjoying a cup of herbal tissane and a chat at the kitchen table when a shadow fell across the window which faced on to the narrow country road. Immersed in semi-darkness the three women stood up to discover what had caused this strange shade and saw the immaculately caparisoned figure of Myra emerge from a long stretch limousine driven by a man in a black peaked hat.

'In the name of Fafnir,' said Angerboda, 'it's Myra. I haven't seen her for years. I wonder what she could want.'

Angerboda had been Queen of the Witches when Myra had seduced Sheenah's husband and, although privately she had disapproved, publicly she had refused to take sides. There was too much controversy and bickering amongst covens anyway. She considered it one of her great achievements as Queen that she had done so much to forge links of understanding in a commonwealth often divided between the opinions of the militant feminists, those who practised skyclad and sex magick, and those of traditional and conservative beliefs. The followers of the Dianic, Alexandrian and Gardnerian traditions were often at philosophical loggerheads, arguing loudly about some fine point of semantics or promoting deeply felt points about obscure pantheons. If there was one thing witches needed, in Angerboda's opinion, it was the strength of unanimity.

Frigga and Freya looked at each other for, unlike their grandmother, they read the newspapers and they had often been exposed to stories about Myra and her activities. With the perspicacity of the true witch Frigga said:

'I bet she's come about the election, Granny.'

Angerboda opened the door.

'Blessed Reverend Rune-Mistress, Queen of the Witches,' said Myra. 'Peace.'

'Peace,' said Angerboda and waved her in. 'What about your – um – man?'

'Oh, he'll be all right. He reads the *Daily Mirror* and goes to sleep.'

Myra presented Angerboda with gifts from London: tonka beans and Black Cohosh, which she knew were hard to find, some heliotrope oil and a plaster bust of the head of Odin, mighty God of the Teutons, that she had found in a Hungerford antique shop. She personally thought the one-eyed Lord of Valhalla suffered from arrested development, but she knew that Angerboda, who hailed from the Nordic mystery tradition, honoured and venerated him.

'It's nice to see you, Myra,' said Angerboda. 'You look as if you've done very well for yourself.'

'Yes,' smiled Myra with what she assumed was girlish modesty. 'I've made some money playing the market.'

'Playing the market? How clever,' said the reigning sovereign of Wicca, poking the fire. 'I've never understood how one does that. It's like betting on the horses, is it?'

'A bit like that, Mother.'

'And how is your son, Cu Cuchulainn?'

'He's fine.'

'And the Sisters of Diana?'

'They're fine. We've become very active within the Green Party, you know.'

'Good.'

Angerboda was appreciative.

'And do you still read the runes, O Queen?'

'Of course,' said Angerboda, who was an acknowledged world expert on the ancient alphabet.

'To what do we owe the pleasure of this visit?' inquired Freya, who wondered how her grandmother could possibly like this over-made-up woman in the bright green suit and gold necklaces.

Sensing someone who was not an ally, Myra flashed her most disarming smile in the direction of Freya who felt an impulse to run for cover in case it contained rays that were carcinogenic.

'Blessed and Most Reverend Matriarch,' purred the visiting High Priestess. 'As you may know I have won the South

33

London by-election and Eumonia of the Daughters of Calatin, who represents the area, has officially announced my candidacy for the Queen of the Witches. I was wondering, O Mother . . .' Myra paused for breath. 'If you would consider proffering your vote on my behalf.'

Angerboda stopped poking the fire and stood up. Her long grey plait hung down her back and she seemed as tall as the giantess of Jotunheim, after whom she was named. With the penetrating blue eyes that are the birthright of those born in the land below Yggdrasil, she looked down on Myra and studied her in silence for some minutes.

Mother of Hel, Myra thought. I've blown it.

'Myra, Mistress of the Stars and Temple Leader of the South London Sisters of Diana,' Angerboda said, 'what do you think you could personally bring to the position of Queen of the Witches?'

Frigga and Freya leaned forward with interest.

'Reverend Measurer, Challenger and Initiator,' said Myra, 'I know full well that I am unworthy to lead the Coven of Covens, but I feel I have been diligent in my magickal work and I have not broken the rules of the Goddess. I have done what I can for my fellow sisters and I feel that She Who Giveth All will help me remain uncorrupted by the power that such a position must surely bestow. I work hard, I have a good image with the press, and I have the best interest of the Craft always in my heart.'

Angerboda nodded. 'Well,' she said, 'although I object to this American-style canvassing that has become fashionable in recent elections, the position certainly requires someone of a strong disposition – mentally, spiritually and physically, especially since the Coven of Covens has become something of a consumer watchdog. We have to deal with all sorts of complaints. There are a lot of frauds out there, you know. Some so-called psychic sisters couldn't predict their way out of Tesco. Every witch who promises to bring green to a garden or health to a herd or contact with dead Auntie Marge, and fails to do so, casts aspersion on the rest of us. The Goddess knows, it is difficult enough as it is. Only the other day, in Chipping Cadbury, a child screamed when it saw me.'

'I know, O Wisdom,' said Myra. 'The Burning Times are gone but the prejudice is still there. I have argued for the

Craft myself on the television. I have appeared in debates at the Oxford Union.'

'I feel,' said Angerboda, 'that the Queen of the Witches must be as strong as Athene, as careful as Themis and as honest as Dike, and I shall certainly consider voting for you, Myra.'

'Oh, thank you,' said Myra, leaping up and kissing her.

'Good,' said Angerboda. 'There are other candidates but it will probably be between you and Sheenah, High Priestess of the Divine Order of Isis.'

The expression of joyous gratitude froze upon Myra's face.

'I was aware,' she said carefully, 'that West London had voted her in. Sheenah is certainly a most powerful and popular Priestess, although, perhaps, a little commercial for my taste . . .'

'It will be a close competition,' said Angerboda, 'and all the better for being so.'

'Granny, really!' said Freya as Myra glided gracefully down the road in her limousine. 'How could you be fooled by a woman like that?'

'What do you mean?'

'Look at her,' Freya continued. 'She's got money coming out of her ears and about as much spirituality as a saveloy.'

'She's a Skogfru,' agreed Frigga, referring to the female forest spirit of Nordic myth who appeared as a beauteous woman but who, from behind, could be seen to be made of dried bark and hollow logs.

'I'm surprised at you both for being so old-fashioned,' retorted the Queen. 'There is too much given to this idea that, just because one is a witch, one has to be an impoverished member of the lunatic fringe. Money is an Empowerer. It creates and it enables. It can be a good thing and in the case of the Queen of the Witches, an appointment which gives access to the Sacred Bank Account, to be wealthy in one's own right would be a helpful defence against temptation. Anyway,' she concluded, putting the tea cups into the sink with a clatter, 'I don't think you should condemn people because they've done well and been on the television.'

'Granny, really,' repeated Freya and glanced at Frigga who, in silent sibling support, was pulling a face behind their grandmother's back.

'And don't pull faces, Frigga,' said Angerboda without looking around.

On the way back to London Myra imagined the live body of Sheenah being turned on a spit over a fire, then sliced into escalopes by painted cannibals who, having tasted her flesh, spat it viciously out on to the jungle floor saying she was too revolting to eat, but the stock would make a useful insecticide.

As the full force of venom surged through Myra's capillaries, the waist-band of her Arabella Pollen skirt cut into her. She loosened the zip with the difficulty of one who has just spent £50 on a French manicure.

That Queen of the Underworld! That maggot! That fat lummox! The world should be grateful she had never bred.

Myra obsessed about her old adversary. Her puerile eccentricities. Her self-conscious philanthropy. Her liberal politics. The fact that she looked as if she got dressed in the dark. She remembered how Sheenah had so pathetically surrendered her husband and then by magical and underhand means (Myra was certain) had caused him to disappear. Well. Harold hadn't been that much of a prize. The hunt had been the thing – the hunt and the kill. If she had had time to notice how dull he was, she might not have bothered to expend the effort.

She had damned him with the Curse of Avengement, not so much because she had been disappointed when he left (he said he was going out for a pint and never came back) but because she had been riled by his nerve. The curse had been effective, apparently. She had heard that Harold was in a charity hospice near Theydon Bois.

Myra knew that although Harold had been easy to wrest from Sheenah's grasp, the post of Queen of the Witches might not be. A high profile counted for much in the run-up to the election. Myra possessed the advantage of fame, but she was also a relative *arriviste* to the circles of witchery and experience was highly rated. Sheenah's grandmother had once represented Wales in the Coven of Covens and, as a hereditary witch, Sheenah enjoyed the support of the rank and file. She was a dangerous opponent.

But she would lose. For Myra's political benefactor was the Prince of Darkness and Chief of the Infernal Empire, the power of whom no soul could contest.

36

CHAPTER FIVE

Rosaleen Arundell was late for the first session of Witchcraft 1 owing to the fact that she had been following Andrew Grateman down the King's Road. He had told her he was spending February in California for tax reasons and she had believed him until, nipping out of the Markham Pharmacy she spotted him walking on the other side of the road. A sighting of Andrew Grateman always caused painful palpitations but, combined with these circumstances of mystery, it presented a challenge that morbid fascination failed to resist.

She wanted to know why he had lied, where he was going and whether women were involved in this constitutional. So as he swanned up the pavement she bobbed surreptitiously after him, leaping strategically into side streets and behind pillar boxes.

He planted himself for half an hour in Picasso eating a *croque monsieur* and drinking cappuccino while she shivered and stamped her feet in the doorway of a shoe shop opposite. Then he sauntered towards World's End stopping at infinite numbers of menswear outlets, emerging from each with a different coloured carrier bag.

She was about to jump out in front of him at the corner of Beaufort Street and pretend it was a coincidence when he turned around. To her embarrassment and dismay she saw that it was not Andrew Grateman at all, but another man whose haircut happened to look similar from the back and who shared Grateman's taste for overcoats designed by Yohji Yamomoto.

By that time it was 6.55 pm. Thoroughly unnerved, she ran all the way back down the King's Road, fell into her Peugeot which was parked outside her house, and drove at reckless speed to Shepherd's Bush where she instantly became lost in the one-way system that wove around the residential streets. When she eventually rang the bell she was flushed and breathing heavily.

Sheenah led her into the temple where three acolytes were sitting drinking tea out of china decorated with cats.

There was a grinning individual with beige trousers and red hair, an etiolated girl whose peasant-style dirndl skirt was teamed with suede moccasin boots and, in the corner in an armchair, one of the most attractive men Rosaleen had ever seen. Dark hair was scraped back from a lupine forehead, black eyes stared from a brown face, and lips curled to reveal slightly snaggle teeth. He was wearing a leather jacket, black Levis and cowboy boots, and he looked as if he was about to spring.

Sheenah introduced them as Cuthbert, Melinda and Steve respectively. Rosaleen, hoping that she hadn't stared at Steve for too long, or that he thought she was red in the face because of him, squashed herself into the sofa beside Cuthbert whose aftershave had obviously arrived in the room long before he had.

Sheenah presented a glamorous if startling figure in a silver caftan embroidered with cabbalistic insignia. There were green stockings on her legs, silver pumps with pom-poms on her feet, and several heavy ankhs around her neck. The silver of the caftan was reiterated in the silver and grey artwork that graced her eyelids (the allergy had finally surrendered). Tachist spots of pink had eased themselves from her lips to her teeth.

'Now,' Sheenah said, 'before we start the slide show, which is the introductory talk to Witchcraft One, I usually ask everyone to tell us a little about themselves so that we can get to know each other. The better we know each other, the more effective we can be as a group. Melinda, why don't you start?'

They turned to face Melinda. Her lank, mouse-coloured hair hung from a centre parting and her pallid skin was gritty in texture. She looked as if she had been recently exhumed.

'My name is Melinda,' she said in a slow, bored tone, 'I am a vegan and a Cancer and I'm into crystals, yeah?'

The last word was somewhere between a speech impediment and a nervous query about her validity.

'And why are you coming to Witchcraft One?' prompted Sheenah helpfully.

The girl sighed. 'I think it's a very interesting subject, yeah? And I would like to find myself.'

'Thank you,' said Sheenah, thinking privately that eighteen steak dinners might help Melinda find herself.

'Rosaleen?'

There was nothing Rosaleen hated more than having attention focussed on her. At school she had sung in a loud and flat voice so she would not be selected to appear in concerts. Her face, still roseate from the efforts of the journey, deepened to fuschia. She looked down at her hands. Her heartbeat and the blood seemed to have disappeared from her throat, causing paralysis in the region of the larynx. She didn't really know why she was sitting on this sofa with this extraordinary silver woman and three strangers, except it was something to do and it might help her get a boyfriend.

Something told her, however, that she should not admit to these facts.

'Hullo,' she said. 'I'm Rosaleen Arundell.' Her voice sounded uncharacteristically breathless, as if she had been watching too many Marilyn Monroe films. 'I'm twenty-three and single. And, um . . . I ride.'

Sheenah turned to the red-haired youth. 'Cuthbert?'

'My name is Cuthbert Cuthbertson and I am interested in the occult.'

'And what do you do, dear?'

'I'm a policeman.'

Rosaleen was a little surprised to hear this confession but her reaction was understated in comparison to that of Steve. Out of the corner of her eye she noticed him sit bolt upright, then, having appreciated that this involuntary reaction could be construed as defensive, he slumped back in the armchair and stared into the middle distance.

Sheenah looked at the dark young man reclining to her right and felt the same sensation she had experienced when he brushed past her to stride through her front door. There was something preternatural about him, preternatural, powerful and strangely familiar.

'I'm Steve,' he said. 'I drive vans.'

Sheenah knew this was not the whole truth, but she had been unable to ascertain his surname as his aloof manner discouraged questions. He was determined, it seemed, to be a mystery.

'And I am Sheenah,' she announced, jewellery jangling. 'High Priestess, Witch, Crone and Hierophant of the Divine Order of Isis. I have been a witch since I was sixteen when, I might add, it was both dangerous and illegal. I hope to teach you some of what I know, so you can learn the truth about witchcraft and go with it into the world where I hope it will support you in everything you choose to do.

'If after three months you find you are still interested in the Craft, you can graduate to Witchcraft Two with a view to being initiated and joining my coven.'

Melinda's eyes were half-closed, Cuthbert was jotting enthusiastically in a spiral-bound notepad, Rosaleen was pretending not to study Steve and Steve was staring with impenetrable black eyes at Sheenah. The experienced witch shuddered.

'Here is some information about the course.' She handed out photocopied folios headlined 'Witchcraft 1'. 'Classes are on Wednesdays and start at seven pm. Punctuality will be appreciated.'

Rosaleen took her copy and noted, with disapointment, that she would have to wait for four weeks to learn spells pertaining to the entrapment of men.

Feb 2:	*Imbolc.*
	(Introduction and slide show on the history of witchcraft.)
Feb 9:	*Meditation and the Sixth Sense.*
Feb 16:	*The Tools of Witchery.*
	(How to make your own wand.)
Feb 23:	*The Altar.*
	(How to make a Protection Spell.)
March 2:	*Magic for Love and Happiness.*
March 9:	*The Goddess and the God.*

'Now,' Sheenah continued 'we have a slide show which tells you about the history of witchcraft and will impress upon you, I hope, that as a minority group we have suffered persecution and massacre. I must warn you that some of the pictures are extremely disgusting. I will tell you when they are due so those of a nervous disposition can put a cushion over your face. Could you turn the lights out please, Cuthbert?'

They settled back into the dark.

'Today,' proclaimed Sheenah from behind the projector, 'February the Second, is known as Imbolc or Candlemas and is one of the ancient pagan festivals celebrated by witches. The other Sabbats are Eostra on March the twenty-first, Beltane on May the first, Midsummer's Night on June the twenty-first, Lammas on August the second, Koré on September the twenty-first and Samhain or Halloween on October the thirty-first. Tonight we are celebrating Saint Brighid, or Bridget, who has come to be known for smithwork, lactation and the world of poetry.'

PC Cuthbertson scribbled furiously about the patron saintess of poems.

'Here is Bridget with her cow.'

Sheenah flicked the switch, the dome clicked around and a fat nun, eyes turned heavenwards, appeared on the screen. She was leaning against a heifer. Another click revealed two fierce men wearing the white collars of Puritanism.

'These are Heinrich Kramer and Jakob Sprenger, authors of *Malleus Maleficarum*, or *The Hammer of the Witches*. The work, commissioned by Pope Innocent the Eighth in 1486, claimed that witches worshipped the Devil and rode goats. As a handbook of torture it was used by witchfinders for two hundred and fifty years.'

Sheenah took her class from Celts and Druids to Gerald Gardner via the Burning Times. She explained that Christians were responsible both for the persecution of an inestimable number of innocent people and for the bad press that witches still received. Half-naked girls in décolleté blouses were flashed on the screen being burned alive or pressed to death between wooden planks weighed down with boulders.

'Are there any questions?' she said as Cuthbert leaped to turn the lights back on.

Suddenly, behind her, came the pad of footsteps.

'Ah,' said Sheenah. 'This is Catty. My familiar.'

Catty stalked past without acknowledging her presence and climbed into the lap of Melinda who emitted a sound like someone who has just received eight bullets in the stomach.

'Oh, I'm so sorry, dear,' said Sheenah. 'Is she heavy?'

'Yes,' muttered the girl, who felt as if several bones had been broken in her legs.

'Catty dear, come to mum,' suggested Sheenah, in the tone she reserved for offering delicious food.

The recumbent animal remained on the lap of Melinda, whose attempts to push her off were thwarted by the fact that the cat's claws had hooked deeply into the fabric of her dirndl skirt.

'Catty, come to mum,' repeated Sheenah a little more sharply. The last thing she wanted was either a scene or a showdown of wills in front of her pupils.

Catty did not move.

'Oh, Jesus!' whispered Sheenah in an uncharacteristically un-Pagan oath.

There was an awkward silence, broken only by Melinda snuffling. Then Steve rose from his seat, went over to Melinda and stared for some time into the cat's face. Catty became

42

still, then she drew back into a ball, leaped off Melinda's lap and ran out of the room.

'God! How did you manage to do that?' exclaimed Rosaleen.

Steve shrugged. 'You just have to know how to handle cats.'

Sheenah, whose relationship with Catty had been based on mutual distrust for many years, knew about cats, but she had never learned how to 'handle' this one. She knew it took a very particular person to do so. A person who knew more about magic than he was prepared to admit. She said nothing but resolved to light a yellow candle and divine the matter later on.

After consuming Sainsbury's wine and the Sabbat biscuits that Sheenah had modified from a recipe for shortbread, the trainee witches filed home. Rosaleen wished she had the courage to offer Steve a lift, but then she saw him loping towards an old Bedford van on which there was a sticker saying 'Elvis is King'. She wondered where he lived and allowed herself to fantasise about him, an activity enhanced by the knowledge that her mother would not approve. Her mother thought that leather jackets were a sign of criminality. Perhaps Steve was a criminal. He had certainly looked most uncomfortable sitting in the same room as a policeman. Perhaps he had been in prison. Rosaleen grew quite excited at the thought and had to turn the heating down in the car.

He had the same air of detachment that she found so compelling about Andrew Grateman. As the implications of this unfortunate similarity impressed themselves upon her, she realised, with cheerless submission, that if he was like Andrew Grateman he was probably repelled by blonde neurotics who longed for commitment.

Still, as she settled down in bed with her copy of *My Mother Myself* she couldn't help looking forward to the next class.

Later that night Sheenah rang Merlin the Magus for a chat and to let him know that she was still alive, despite Mars and Saturn.

'Darling,' said Merlin. 'How are the students?'

'Well, put it this way: two out of four look inept rather than adept.'

'What about the little one I sent along from my shop?'

'Rosaleen? Honestly, Merlin, I don't know where you find them. I fear for the girl's safety, really I do. She's as dizzy as a top and obsessed by men.'

'Aren't we all?' said Merlin.

'There's one I'm worried about. I feel that I've seen him before and I'm sure he's no newcomer. He hypnotised Catty.'

'Cailleach's Cauldron!' expostulated Merlin. 'He's certainly no newcomer.'

'He's also very handsome. You'll like him . . . but they're always the worst. I think Rosaleen's got her eyes on him.'

'She did tell me she was looking for a boyfriend,' said Merlin.

'I was hoping,' observed the votary of Isis, 'that this was going to be a serious course for those interested in becoming initiated into the Craft rather than some occult singles group.'

'Don't worry,' said Merlin. 'Listen, I'm afraid I've got some bad news for you. I was going to ring earlier but I had to go and help William the Warlock paint his kitchen – apricot, can you believe? – and I forgot.'

Sheenah looked at her watch. It was 11.46 pm. Mars still opposed Saturn. She sighed.

'You have a rival for Queen of the Witches.'

'I'm bound to have rivals. There are always at least four nominees.'

'No, but this is bad.'

'Who is it?'

Merlin breathed out heavily. 'Myra.'

This horrible announcement rendered Sheenah incapable of speech. It was not that she was overwhelmed by the prospect of a confrontation, but thinking of Myra lead to thinking about Harold, a memory that she had conscientiously banned from her mind, aware, always, of its dangerous effect on her psyche.

Merlin continued. 'What's more, it looks as if she might have Angerboda's vote,' he said. 'Her granddaughter Freya told me. Myra went down there today in a stretch limo. The whole village is talking about it. Apparently they thought it was Elton John. Anyway, Angerboda fell victim to the charms of Myra's canvassing.'

44

'She's always liked Myra,' said Sheenah quietly. 'Well I suppose that's it, then. I'll have to accept the Goddess's will, and hope I don't lose too badly.'

'You'll do no such thing,' Merlin argued. 'Myra might be in a strong position, particularly if Angerboda does vote for her because many members of the Coven of Covens will follow her lead, but she would be a heinous Queen of the Witches. It's more important than ever before that you win this election. The Craft needs you. Myra's numbers are wrong for this job. She's power-crazed and could wreak havoc. We have to do everything we can to make sure you win. You'll have to mount a campaign and canvass as aggressively as she does, that's all. And if it requires photo opportunities and open-top cars and rosettes and publicity, then that's what you'll have to do.'

Sheenah put down the telephone, poured herself a glass of brandy and went to bed.

It was going to be a tough contest.

CHAPTER SIX

The third session of Witchcraft 1 fell in the same week as St
Valentine's Day. This was always a traumatic date for Rosaleen, worse even than Christmas. This year she had desisted
from her custom of sending anonymous bunches of flowers to
herself, but not from dispatching a blizzard of cards to others.

The morning was spent, nose pressed against the window,
waiting for the postman, wondering if Andrew Grateman
would appreciate the velour heart she had sent to his address
in Pacific Palisades, and praying for a sign of a sympathetic
response. By about 12.30 the stirrings in her breast had exhausted her. She was about to pour a consoling Campari and
orange juice when the letter box lid clinked and the mail
slapped on to the hall floor.

Rosaleen hurdled an umbrella stand and fell on two envelopes. One turned out to be a circular. The other was a
pink envelope decorated with small disjointed handwriting.
She ripped it open with shaking and gleeful hands to find a
lurid photograph of a couple with Seventies hairstyles walking at sunset along a beach. Inside an embarrassing message
composed in swirled gold letters suggested she should belong
to the nameless sender until the end of time. It certainly
wasn't from Andrew Grateman. Assuming it must be a joke
from one of her more ghastly friends, she checked the post-
mark. W12. She didn't know anyone who lived in Shepherd's
Bush apart from the BBC and Sheenah of the Divine Order
of Isis, and it couldn't be from either of them.

Two days later, Sheenah showed the class her besoms and
bollines and devoted the last hour of the lecture to emphas-
ising the importance of the wand.

'The wand,' she said, 'is the most vital piece of equipment. It is charged with the owner's energy so no one else can gain power from it, and it is indispensable to all spells. It doesn't really matter what you use to make one although, of course, it should be wood. The most effective is hazel because it is ruled by Mercury, the planet of knowledge, and ideally it should be cut by an athame at midnight of the first full moon after the winter solstice when the sun has entered the sign of Capricorn. Since we are now in February, you have missed that and will have to make do with what you can. However, I do advise you to consecrate them at the next full moon at midnight, which I think' – she paused to consult her Astrology Association diary – 'is at the beginning of next week.'

Then she handed them photocopied sheets on which the prayer of consecration to 'Charge All Wandes of Witchery' had been written.

Rosaleen looked up from the ancient stanza to catch Cuthbert staring at her. His features were arranged into a grin which revealed no teeth and looked as if it had been drawn on to his face by a cartoonist. When she gazed back he did not avert his eyes, abashed, as most people would, but continued to inspect her in a way that was both knowing and disconcerting.

Crikey, she thought. I hope that Valentine wasn't from him.

Rosaleen, unlike many women, was not attracted by the idea of uniforms and handcuffs. Romantic involvement with a policeman, in her opinion, would bring with it all sorts of liabilities and disadvantages, and the onus not to break the law was only one of them. Her mind moved involuntarily to her broken brake light and the fact that her road tax was out of date. He was bound to notice.

She flushed guiltily and turned away from PC Cuthbertson to look at Steve, whose appearance was particularly elevating this evening.

The aura of the spellbinding Steve had also been noticed by Sheenah, who attempted to focus magically into it in order to perceive the secrets of his spirit. Her efforts were unsuccessful and she realised, with a shock, that he was surrounded by an invisible force field that prohibited the seeking of paranormal information about his personality. The technique was

47

one of advanced mastery and could only be known by one versed in the occult arts.

She continued on the subject of wands.

'I have here,' she said, holding up a small brown stick, 'one that I made myself when I was a junior witch. It has served me well over the years. But this is my best one.' She displayed a long mahogany staff whose base was carved with silver and ornamented with glass beads. 'I use this for my powerful magic. It is supposed to be very old and was used, I have been told, to raise the cone of power during the Gardnerian ceremony to prohibit Adolf Hitler from landing on these shores. This was a ritual that was so strenuous that some elderly witches died soon afterwards. It worked though, didn't it?' she said, gazing around the room.

'Sometimes,' she went on, 'I think I can magic anything up with this wand, although if I said that you'd ask me why I haven't conjured up pots of money for myself.'

She laughed, threw the wand into the air and caught it again like a majorette.

'So why haven't you?' inquired Steve.

'Well,' replied the High Priestess, who was not ashamed of her impecuniosity and therefore had no emotional difficulty discussing it, 'I'm simply not interested, to tell you the truth. I have so much to do with the Witches' League, the healing, the reading and Catty that I've never really focused on the business side of things. Consequently I've always had more than enough. The Goddess' – she indicated the portrait of Isis on the temple door – 'makes sure we get what we need when we need it.

'Now this week's project is for you all to make yourselves a wand and bring it to the next class, when we will be learning how to set up an altar and how to mix a Protection spell so our enemies cannot harm us.'

At this last sentence she gazed at Steve with an expression of what she hoped was superior discernment. She could see nothing in his black eyes except the light of the candles dancing in them, but she sensed that if she lingered there objectivity would fail her and, in some way, she would be led by him. She glanced down at her notes and up again and saw that he was smiling to himself.

Rosaleen noticed this subtle interaction and wondered if Sheenah fancied Steve as well.

'So did you get any Valentines then, Ros?' said Cuthbert as she was unlocking her car door. She stood up and leaned unconvincingly over the icy bonnet in an effort to hide her out-of-date road tax disc, which, because it was on the other side of the window, meant she looked like a pine tree in a hurricane. 'Um, yes,' she grunted, the contortion making it difficult to breathe. 'I did, actually. Did you?'

'Might 'ave done.' He smirked with infuriating familiarity. 'Might 'ave done.'

'Um, do you live near here, then?'

'Yeah. The section house is round the corner. It's handy for the station, see?'

'Ah,' said Rosaleen. 'Well. 'Night then.'

'You should get that brake light fixed. It's a bit dodgy,' he said, and marched off down the street.

'Christ,' muttered Rosaleen. 'So it was him. Bloody hell!'

In normal circumstances she would have fretted about this incident. She would have imagined appalling scenes in which she was forced to attend policemen's balls and she would have flailed around in a mental maze searching for the correct methods of repelling advances made by Her Majesty's keepers of the peace. But her mother began ringing her at hourly intervals to inquire if she had found a tenant for the basement flat yet and this offensive was supported by letters from trustees and Coutts bank, all of whom were unafraid to remind her that the magnitude of her overdraft was causing them deep personal anxiety.

The estate agent sent crowds of people around, and there were the usual remarks about how dark basements were. Was it a shared garden? Was that damp in the corner of the kitchenette? Wasn't it funny how yellow always reminded one of hospitals? When the day of the next class came round she had completely forgotten about the wand until it was nearly time to leave for Shepherd's Bush.

Rosaleen rushed around the house looking for something that would do. A wand-like shape that would suffice for the making of magic.

49

I bet PC Cuthbertson has got hazel, consecrated at midnight and all, she thought darkly to herself. Flaming teacher's pet.

She didn't think that the handle of the dish-mop was suitable, nor the horns that were pressed into the rows of Manolo Blahnik shoes, nor the prickly thing that was designed to clean the loo. So in a panic she drove to the General Trading Company ten minutes before it was due to close.

'Good evening, madam,' said a middle-aged, streamlined shop assistant who emphasised the evening part of this salutation. 'Have you come about a wedding list?'

I wish, thought Rosaleen

'No,' she said.

'Can I help at all?' said the woman, glancing at her watch with the assiduous eye of someone who needed to catch the 7.10 to Enfield if she was to be back in time to cook dinner for a family of three.

'I'll know it when I see it,' Rosaleen said firmly, and skirted past her like a mouse avoiding a chair leg. She jogged through departments full of engraved glassware and dhurries, wooden ducks, apple-scented guest soaps, embroidered cushion covers and pricey objects carved by Mexicans.

Eventually she came to a corner in which there was a range of flowers constructed from feathers, fabric and wire. This copse was so cunningly crafted, with its moss and leaves and bark, that the geraniums and roses seemed as if they were growing in it.

Perfect, she said plucking a stalk with a frothy silken head. I'll remove the top and use the stem. It looks exactly like Sheenah's.

It wasn't until she unwrapped the hand-made blossom in the car that she noticed the stalk was plastic artfully painted to look like authentic nature. She wondered if plastic would do, and suspected that it would not. The optical illusion was convincing, though. Perhaps no one would notice the difference.

Steve answered the door. He had the mien of someone who was about to dare you to do something frightening and possibly immoral. Rosaleen wondered, fleetingly, if he was armed.

'Hullo,' he said, black eyes amused. 'You're late again.'

She paused for a minute on the doorstep, waiting for him to give way so that her chest would not brush against his as she entered the house.

'I know,' she said. 'I'm sorry.'

'I don't expect we'll explode.'

He stood aside to let her through, closed the door behind her and motioned her to lead the way down to the temple. This sequence of old-fashioned courtesy surprised her. His leather jacket did not advertise gallantry and neither did his gait, which was the slow stride of a man unworried by the strictures of time. She had assumed that Steve would not have any manners and she realised, with a pang of mortification, that she was wrong.

Sheenah had backcombed her hair into a beehive which meant that she had to turn her head with a certain amount of care. This precarious balancing act was further complicated by the hanging of gold Christmas tree decorations in her ears which plinked like wind chimes. The full effect, above the neck, was akin to kinetic sculpture. Below the neck, however, welled a different story. A full-length robe of many blues cascaded over her, so that when her large chest heaved up and down to allow oxygen to enter the thorax, the light refracted on the folds created the illusion of a waterfall.

'Now,' she proclaimed, 'the first thing we do this evening is to cast a circle and charge your wands. The anomaly with wands and circles is that you need a wand to cast a circle, but you can't charge a wand without a circle. We're okay because mine is charged, of course, and has been for years. Whatever you do, do not break the circle. That is very, very dangerous. And try not to make any loud noises for this can destroy our concentration and decrease the power of our magic.'

She looked at Melinda as she said this, for the withered girl was coughing as if she was about to choke to death.

'I'll get some of my special bugleweed linctus,' Sheenah said gently and flowed to the kitchen.

Poor Melinda. Her skin looked like a paperback that has been read during a holiday on the beach. Her hair was lanker than ever, her neck seemed incapable of supporting her head so her chin pressed itself into her chest, and she seemed to have lost even more weight. The bony knots of her elbows jutted underneath the sleeves of her Biba scoop-neck T-shirt and one could see her collar bones, unnaturally fleshless, rising up and down as the paroxysms gripped her body.

51

Cuthbert – whose wand, as Rosaleen had predicted, was made out of hazel and had been consecrated under the light of the full moon – was wearing a new pentacle around his neck.

Steve held a simple varnished stick that looked ordinary to the lay-person, but Sheenah knew it was hawthorn and, judging from the fact that it was decorated with the magical alphabet from the Key of Solomon, it was also old, very old, possibly a possession that had been handed down from one witch to another over many generations. Perhaps this was the answer. Steve came from a family of witches. It would explain his advanced mysticism, but not why he had ventured on her course.

'Rosaleen,' said Sheenah, pointing with a long gold finger-nail towards the front of the altar, 'that is north. Please take this sea salt and sprinkle it clockwise over the nine-foot circle you will see marked in light chalk. When you have done this, walking in the same direction, make another two circles, one inside the other.'

Then Sheenah gave Cuthbert a thurible and instructed him how to swing it without allowing the lid to fly off causing a shower of burning coals to rain upon the assembly.

Slowly the class followed Rosaleen clockwise around the sea salt chanting:

By spirit and earth, by fire and sea
Guard this circle, so mote it be.

Then they stood around the altar, holding hands. Rosaleen was pleased to find Steve on her right, but less enchanted to feel Cuthbert's moist digits insinuating themselves from the left.

Sheenah lit the incense and candles, and as the temple filled with the bitter aroma of frankincense her solemn mega-phonic tones echoed through the flickering penumbra.

'I Sheenah, High Priestess and Mother of the Divine Order of Isis, cast this circle to protect us from all harmful forces. I charge this circle to attract only harmony and peace.'

Then she invited a pantheon of divinities, ondines and saintly emanations to join them.

As the Priestess invoked the goodly powers of Isis and her kin, an electric shock shot through Rosaleen and she realised that Steve's hand, initially cool and firm, was now pulsing with heat.

Sheenah told them to remain where they were, but to put their wands in their right hands and close their eyes. She directed them to study their wands with their minds for any vile energies that could obstruct the path of their magic, and to clear them away with the forces of thought.

Rosaleen studied her wand, and found she could only think of the shop assistant at the General Trading Company.

Sheenah's voice seemed to resonate from another room.

'Say these things after me,' it bade. 'I charge this wand . . .'

'I charge this wand,' they all chanted.

'To catalyse my every thought, word and deed by my will.'

'To catalyse my every thought, word and deed by my will.'

'So mote it be.'

'So mote it be.'

Surprised into confusion by this abnormal ceremony, Rosaleen opened her eyes from a mixture of nerves and curiosity. The figures standing around the candle-lit altar all represented somnambulists except Melinda, who was purple from the effort of trying to contain her coughing against the nimbulae of incense billowing into her face.

Sheenah continued the serious task of imparting the knowledge of the Ancient Mysteries and, aware of the importance of drama in the teaching process, availed herself of the husky magniloquence of a command performance.

'The tool,' she told them, 'becomes a magical object capable of carrying out spells. Each of you may walk deosil, clockwise, around the circle and touch the statue of the Goddess Isis with your consecrated wand. As you do so, say, "I, Child of the Goddess, pray that She, the Goddess, may grant . . ." and what you want. Then say, "I ask that this be correct and for the good of all." And we all join in with "So mote it be." '

They walked around the circle. Steve tapped the head of the statue with his wand and said:

'I, Steve, Child of the Goddess, pray that She may grant me wisdom and that this be for the good of all. So mote it be.'

'So mote it be.'

'I, Cuthbert, Child of the Goddess, pray that She may grant that I pass my exams in September and I ask that this may be correct and for the good of all. So mote it be.'

'So mote it be.'

'I, Melinda, Child of the Goddess, pray that She may grant me £10,000 to expand my business and that this may be for the good of all. So mote it be.'

'So mote it be.'

Rosaleen, albeit swayed by the psycho-dramatics of this pageant, did not feel confident enough to impart her innermost feelings and admit to a temple full of student witches that it was not money she sought, or even beauty, but a fiancé.

She compromised.

'I, Rosaleen, Child of the Goddess, pray that She may grant somebody to rent my basement flat so that my mother will shut up. So mote it be.'

'So mote it be.'

'You forgot to say that you ask for it to be for the good of all,' said Sheenah. 'This is very important, everybody. The astral is full of nasty entities. I've seen things you wouldn't believe, and these words are your insurance policy against the attraction of their malevolent energy.'

Rosaleen looked terrified.

'Never mind,' the witch said. 'I'm sure it will be all right.'

She glided around the altar, festoons of blue waves following behind her, and, waving her small everyday wand in the air, declared that the circle was now open but not unbroken.

They sat down in the chairs. Cuthbert wrote some notes. Rosaleen gawped at her ersatz wand as if sparks might fly out of the top of it.

Sheenah embarked on the second part of her lecture – 'How to make a Protection Pourri'.

'Protection is essential,' she said. 'The ancients used to make Loricas to defend themselves and it is one of the basic elements of witchcraft.'

'Didn't do them much good in the sixteenth century,' observed Steve.

Sheenah ignored him and continued. 'Witches,' she said, 'realise that a certain amount of suffering is one of the inevitabilities of life . . .'

An image of Harold arrived suddenly and without warning into her mind. She dismissed it nervously, but as a powerful dream can colour a day so this picture of her ex-husband clung to her perception.

54

She went on: 'Witches are not people to be pushed and shoved by the Fates. We are not victims. So we use our magic, our knowledge of the ethereal powers, to maintain balance and harmony in our lives. Should harmful vibrations appear to be directed towards us, we believe in active resistance. That is, we know the techniques to neutralise the energy without harming anybody. The witches' law is that whatever you send out comes back to you threefold, and this applies to both good and evil forces.

'The Protection Pourri will help to maintain this balance and harmony and neutralise the mistakes you will undoubtedly make whilst traversing your Wiccan path. It is a very old spell handed down to me by my grandmother whose own mother gave it to her. It might be best if you write the ingredients in your notebooks.'

Four heads bent obediently forward to concentrate on the recording of the antique recipe.

'Six drops of frankincense oil. One teaspoon of dried red clover. A sprig of rosemary. Thirteen hairs from a live wolf. Half a handful of dried pulsatilla leaves. A small pinch of sea salt.

'Mix the ingredients, bind them with the oil, place the mixture in a muslin bag similar to those used for bouquet garni and hang it on your door. Keep it out of the reach of children and animals, for it should not be eaten.'

'Where,' inquired Rosaleen, 'do we get the ingredients?'

'I have some pulsatilla, the rest can be found in those Indian shops in the Portobello Road.'

'And the hair from a live moulting wolf?'

'Well,' said the instructress, 'that is your first real test and the one that gives the Protection Spell its efficacy.'

Rosaleen did not reply that she thought she would need more than efficacy to protect herself against the masticating jaws of a live wolf.

'Wouldn't an alsatian do?' asked Cuthbert, who had easy access to them.

'No,' said Sheenah.

The next morning Sheenah glanced at the back of her kitchen door and noticed, with horror, that her own Protection Spell had disappeared from the place where it had hung for twenty years. There was even a discoloured mark where the sun had bleached the surrounding paintwork. A search revealed nothing. Discomfited, she went into the garden to feed the birds and saw that the robin, who had stoically survived the ravages and freeze of winter and who had comforted her through the dark evenings with the knowledge that it was her grandmother, was lying dead on the table.

This, surely, was an omen.

Tears rolling down her face, Sheenah lifted the lifeless body in her hand and as the damp feathers pricked her palm she experienced the same sensations that had chilled her the day that Granny Maldwyn had died, and the day that Harold had deserted her.

Apprehension. Self-doubt. Demoralisation. Isolation.

The day displayed a more benevolent attitude towards Rosaleen.

She opened her front door to a vision of drain-pipe jeans, a long emerald-green velvet overcoat, and a pair of cheekbones. He was about twenty-five, he had a tattoo on his hand and he was fantastic.

His name was Dig and he had heard that her basement flat was vacant.

They went downstairs and Dig (who said he was a freelance graphic designer) mooched about looking under the kitchen sink at the plumbing, checking the central heating and so on.

'It's still available, then, is it?' he asked.

'Yes,' said Rosaleen. 'You can move in any time you like.'

His suitcases appeared at tea-time.

This magic certainly does work, Rosaleen thought to herself, remembering her spell from the previous evening and eyeing her artificial wand with new respect. But the wolf's hair is a problem. She wondered if the RSPCA would help, or whether there were specialists in this field.

She searched under W in the Yellow Pages but there was only Word Processing and Weight Watching, and nothing to do with wolves at all.

Then her telephone rang.

' 'Ullo, Ros.'

She didn't immediately know who it was.

56

'It's Cuthbert.'

'Oh. Hullo, Cuthbert. How are you?'

'Fine. Ros, I've been thinking about this wolf's hair prob.'

'So have I.'

'Well,' he continued in the clear but unstructured inflection that signified one who was born in South London and who is destined to read things from notebooks in a way that can be understood by benches of local magistrates, 'I've made inquiries and sources have revealed to me that there are wolves in Regents Park Zoo.'

'Are there? I hadn't thought of that.'

'Yes. So I suggest we go there and see what we can do.'

'Fine,' said Rosaleen, her heart sinking slightly at the idea of this enforced date with PC Cuthbertson.

'I'm off Saturday,' he concluded. 'Shall I come and pick you up? O ten hundred hours all right?'

'Okay. Thank you very much.'

Later she went to see if Dig had settled in. He had. So, she couldn't help noticing, had three Rastafarians men who were stationed in front of the television amidst beer cans, ashtrays and newspapers of the small and lying variety. The telephone rang continuously despite the fact that her tenant had only been installed for four hours.

Then she caught sight of his fine angular profile, illuminated by the flicker of the television screen. She saw the way his long fingers shyly pushed his hair back off his face and the fact that his shoes were hand-made. Somehow she knew everything would be OK.

'Take care,' he said, and sniffed.

'Have you got a cold?' she asked kindly.

'Yeah. It's the weather and I've bin living out of a suitcase for a bit. Y'know how it is.'

Rosaleen, who had never lived out of a suitcase in her life, didn't.

'Make sure the heating is up nice and high,' she advised, 'and call me if you need anything – anything at all.'

'Yeah. Okay. Thanks. 'Night, then.'

'Good night,' she said, and was glad that she had put so much make-up on.

57

CHAPTER SEVEN

Cuthbert arrived at o ten hundred hours precisely. Rosaleen, whose hairbrush had become stuck in her hair, told him to help himself to anything he wanted in the kitchen. She joined him twenty minutes later, after an ineffective struggle had forced her to cut the brush out with nail scissors. Having discarded his fawn driving coat with toggle buttons and his leather driving gloves with decorative holes and contrasting stitches, he had made himself a cup of tea and was sitting reading a copy of *The Job*.

'What made you decide to be a policeman, Cuthbert?' she asked politely.

'Well my dad was one, and my granddad. I didn't really want to join the force, then my brother Clive was killed in an RTA and I felt kind of obliged to carry on the family tradition.'

'RTA?'

'Yeah. He was a probationer. The traffic lights went down in Piccadilly and he happened to be on his way to his beat in Covent Garden. He was wearing his uniform, so he leaped out into the middle of the road waving, and a lorry flattened him.'

'I've always thought directing traffic was frightfully dangerous,' sympathised Rosaleen, pouring him out another cup of tea.

'Yeah. Keen our Clive, but not brainy. Anyway the folks were cut up, as you can imagine. I was sixteen and they kept looking at me expectantly. Then I got the O level so I thought all right then.'

'Do you like it?'

'Sometimes I do, sometimes I don't. The money isn't bad and it's got prospects. It'll be better when I transfer to the Dog Section.'

They left the house.

' 'Ere,' said Cuthbert. 'What's that?'

Rosaleen looked down the stone steps that led into her basement flat and saw that there was a queue of some nineteen people up to the front door. They had obviously been there for some time despite the biting easterly wind. One or two had upturned cardboard boxes and were playing cards on them, some had flasks and blankets, but most were smoking and shuffling their feet.

'Goodness,' said Rosaleen. 'That's my new tenant. He must be popular.'

PC Cuthbertson raised his eyebrows but said nothing.

They drove to Regents Park Zoo in Cuthbert's car. A chocolate-coloured Ford Escort, it had a pair of plastic handcuffs hanging from the mirror, nylon seat protectors and smelled of orange air freshener.

'Are you certain they've got wolves?' asked Rosaleen. 'Perhaps we should have gone to Windsor Safari Park.'

'They 'ave,' said Cuthbert. 'I double-checked.'

'Did you double-check about their eating habits?'

'I thought further questioning as to the nature of the animals' diet might be a little suspicious,' he said. 'We're going to 'ave to be dead careful anyway. If I get nicked doing anyfing improper it'll be serious dos. I could be thrown out of the force.'

'Dear me,' said Rosaleen. 'Are you sure you should be risking it?'

He shrugged. 'We've got to have the hair, haven't we?'

'I suppose so. But do you think Sheenah could tell if we got bits of fluff off the carpet or something?'

'She might not be able to tell, Ros, but it wouldn't be magic, would it?'

'You believe in magic, then?'

He shifted gear and she moved her leg out of the way.

'Yeah,' he said. 'Don't you?'

'I do believe there are invisible forces,' she said. 'Forces that we don't know anything about, but I never really thought they could be manipulated by the individual. Now . . .' She thought of the invocation to the Goddess and the subsequent arrival of Dig. 'Now I don't know.'

It took them some time to find the wolves owing to the fact that nobody who worked at the zoo knew where they were and Cuthbert made innumerable detours to look at assorted wildlife. Rosaleen was forced to stare for ages at tanks full of shovelnose sturgeons and Spanish ribbed newts.

'Come on, Ros,' he insisted, pushing her out of the Aquarium and towards the Reptile House, 'might as well look at the boas while we're here.'

And so they gazed at that section of the animal kingdom whose lifestyle has never been handicapped by lack of legs. They passed the North American hog-nosed snake which, when attacked, lies with its tongue hanging out of its mouth and pretends to be dead. They discovered that those of dullest colour were also the most dangerous. The small grey tiger snake, for instance, is known to have attacked people on golf courses in Sydney. And then there was the black mamba, not black at all but olive brown, with grinning mouth and dead eyes and coffin-shaped head. Agile and angry and capable of speeds in excess of twelve mph, the mamba murders (a notice informed them) by causing the victim to choke on his own vomit. Or die of a heart attack. Or both. Finally, in the last cage, a huge Burmese python coiled in the shadows of a man-made stalagmite.

'Blimey,' said Cuthbert, impressed. 'They've been known to swallow children whole.'

A small girl, whose forehead had been pressed against the glass, looked up at him, back at the Burmese assassin and shot away as if she had been fired from a cannon.

'Let's go, Cuthbert,' Rosaleen urged.

Reluctantly, the policeman dragged himself away and they skirted the penguins dipping into an unsightly swimming pool and a hippo in a house that resembled something erected in the Sixties, damned in the Seventies and listed in the Eighties at the suggestion of somebody closely related to the architect. They passed the Big Cats and Pheasants of the World and reached an aviary full of black crested buntings and St Helena seed-eaters.

Then a man addressed them.

'Hullo,' he said.

Rosaleen wheeled around.

60

'Hullo,' he said again.

'Hullo,' she repeated.

'Hullo.'

'Hullo, where are you?'

This was answered by a wolf-whistle and a woman's voice joined in.

'Hullo!' she trilled.

'Hullo,' said Rosaleen.

'Can I get you a drink?' inquired the invisible female.

'No, thank you.'

Rosaleen peered into the bird cage.

Cuthbert screamed with laughter and poked her in the arm.

'They're mynah birds. Stewpid.'

The voices continued the uncanny non-avian conversation amongst themselves.

Rosaleen and Cuthbert (still laughing) turned a corner. In front of them four wolves lay across a rock. The cage was marked with signs saying, 'Wolf Wood', and 'These Animals Are Dangerous'.

The wolves did not appear to be dangerous.

They did not appear to be alive.

They sprawled with their eyes closed. If they did move, it was with narcoleptic lethargy in order to stretch before lying down again. Around them flocks of birds pecked with fearless confidence at large bleeding slabs of meat.

'At least they're not hungry,' said Rosaleen, comforted by the carnivores' similarity to fireside rugs.

'Yeah,' said Cuthbert. 'And look.'

He pointed to another sign which said, 'Wolves often hunt in packs, but despite their bad reputation they virtually never attack people.'

'I'm not keen on the word "virtually",' Rosaleen remarked.

The wolf cage, on closer inspection, did not present an insurmountable challenge to the intruder. The cage was open at the top. One side of the flimsy wire netting opened out into Regents Park and a tarmac jogging track. There were no dissuasive points, no barbed or electrified wire to prevent one from climbing over the top and dropping down on to the ground.

Rosaleen and Cuthbert sequestered themselves in the restaurant to discuss the operation and eat lunch off plastic

61

trays. Rosaleen bought vegetarian lasagne and salad, very expensive, and Cuthbert chose beefburgers, chips, a slice of chocolate fudge cake, a cup of tea and three sugars.

'So what are we going to do?' said Rosaleen, who hardly dared hear the answer.

'Right. I noticed that there is no wolf hair caught on the branches or netting,' said Cuthbert, 'so unfortunately we're going to have to actually go up to one and cut a bit off.'

'What?' she shouted.

'I don't see what else we can do.'

The 'we' sounded ominous.

Rosaleen lunged a plastic knife at him. 'And this, I suppose, will come in useful.'

'I've got these,' said Cuthbert, and produced a Swiss knife on which there was a pair of minute nail scissors.

'What if one of them bites your face off?'

'Those things don't look as if they've ever bitten anything in their lives. The thing is to do it very fast, drop in there, run at them and run out again before they've even noticed anything. The element of surprise, you see. Very effective. We're taught it in Human Awareness at Hendon.'

Rosaleen felt a heavy force depress her whole body.

'When?'

'When the zoo closes at four.'

'It'll be dark.'

'Exactly. I've got a torch.'

'They might be in bed.'

'We'll approach from the park side where those joggers were, so whatever happens we don't have to trespass until the last minute.'

They wandered around looking at lynxes until the zoo closed, then walked round the park until they found themselves outside the wolf cage.

The 'Wolf Wood' was lit by a pink light from one corner, and they could distinguish various lupine shapes in the gloom. The pack had been moved into a night cage and the animals were now sitting around a pool of water looking, Rosaleen was dismayed to observe, much livelier than they had in daylight.

The evening chill bit into her feet, and she shivered.

'Right,' said Cuthbert. 'You stand in that corner and hold the light so I can see. I'll need both me 'ands to get up.'

This was a mistake. She knew it.

'Are you sure?'

'Yeah. Come on, it'll be a breeze. Speed, speed is the secret.'

Heart thudding and body shaking, she climbed over the fence and standing outside the cage, she directed the beam on to the corner in which the wolves were lying. The shard of light turned their eyes into infra-red orbs. One or two swung their tongues lasciviously.

Cuthbert climbed the flimsy wire-mesh behind them, confidence fuelled by the impression that this task was being undertaken in silence. To Rosaleen it sounded as if a fourteen-piece orchestra had arrived and was treating the auditorium to a symphony written by an avant-garde composer whose musical opus encompassed the use of oil drums, electric drills and milk bottles.

Having reached the top Cuthbert let himself fall to the ground. The impact of his barge-sized black boots emitted a thud but the wolves did not seem to hear. He dashed at the group, snipped at the tail of the largest, put the fur in his pocket and ran back to the wire.

One of the wolves raised itself heavily from its supine position and slowly followed him.

'Christ!' hissed Rosaleen. 'Look out behind you.'

Cuthbert leaped up on to the frame but found, to his alarm, that climbing out was a great deal more difficult than climbing in because the wire curved inwards at the top.

'Hullo,' said a male voice.

'Fuck! Somebody's coming,' Rosaleen almost screeched.

'It's the bloody mynah,' grunted Cuthbert, boots sliding helplessly up and down the walls of his prison.

'Hullo,' said the voice again.

Cuthbert continued struggling.

'Stop right there, sonny.'

This was not the message of a feathered species indigenous to Nepal Hill, nor would a mynah bird be capable of shining a torch on to the body of Cuthbert, which was hanging like a bat from the inside of the cage.

The wolves, alert now and interested, circled beneath him.

63

'What the hell do you think you're doing?'

The man with the torch was wearing a blue uniform. Over the right pocket was embroidered the information, 'London Zoo: Night Warden'.

It was evident that Cuthbert was not in a position to explain himself so Rosaleen walked around the cage to where the warden was standing.

'Um, he's dropped something in there. He's just trying to get it out,' she said.

The warden produced a bunch of keys and opened the cage door.

'You'd better come out this way,' he said wearily. 'And try not to let the animals out if at all possible.'

The London Zoo night warden took his job very seriously. He was sixty-one years old and was aware that if he lost it he was unlikely to be offered another one.

He marched them into his office and rang the police.

Cuthbert sank into a chair like a bag of potatoes.

'That's it,' he said morosely. 'I'm done for. I've lost me job, me career, everything.'

There was some confusion among the officers on duty at Albany Street Police Station. They could not see how Cuthbert could have dropped an object into the wolf cage. Where was this object? And what was it? Nothing had been stolen, so Section 9 of the Theft Act did not apply. The suspects had not caused criminal damage, nor even a breach of the peace. This left only trespassing, which was a civil offence. Eventually, after two difficult hours in separate interview rooms, it came to light that Cuthbert was a police constable.

This changed everything.

The matter would have to be dealt with internally. A Sergeant Brady informed the deflated Cuthbert that his super would be given a full report of his night's activities. As for the young lady, since she had no previous and had not actually been in the cage, she could go with a verbal.

Cuthbert was so upset that his driving gloves shook all over the wheel of the Ford Escort and Rosaleen had to take over.

'My life,' he said, bottom lip quivering, 'has come to an end.'

CHAPTER EIGHT

Superintendent Starkweather broke the filter off the end of one of the duty-free John Player Specials that Detective Sergeant Panzram had bought back from an unfruitful attempt to track down 'Big' Bernard Barker in Marbella. Starkweather reflected that if he had followed the instincts of his youth and become a Lord of the Underworld he too would probably be enjoying life on the Costa del Sol. He had not, unfortunately, been quite brave enough and despite a good and exciting year spent removing the lead from church roofs around Swindon he had eventually come up against the Bunt Brothers. Rather than spend the rest of his days wondering when a piece of wood with a nail in it was going to come into contact with the side of his head, he surrendered the exhilaration of sociopathic activity for the easier life on a home beat. Thanks to his intimate knowledge of local villains and his uncanny perceptions about the nature of their minds, he rose quickly through the uniformed ranks, earning a record for arrests at Swindon Police Station that, to his knowledge, had not yet been beaten.

He stubbed the JPS out into the ashtray that one of his ex-wives had bought back from Brighton and stared moodily out of the window into the Uxbridge Road. It was 5.30 am. No one was up except for those paid to preserve public safety, those paid to clear public dust and those paid to cure public diseases. He thought of his happy years with the regional crime squad and the legends of criminal genius they had brought to justice. He wished that some of them would escape so he could have the pleasure of chasing them again – Louis Frotteur, the French sex maniac, Red Foley the armed robber, and Porick O'Connor the Irish con-man. Porick still wrote to him from Springhill. The Super would like it there, he said. A man could learn a lot.

It wasn't that Shepherd's Bush was quiet. Far from it. But it was not him out there fighting the yardies and football fans. It was not him out there riding the horses up and down the Uxbridge Road and making conversation with maniacs on the Green. It was younger, luckier men. Men who had not made the mistake of being promoted.

Another Monday morning.

He rustled around on his desk and felt almost dead from ennui.

Nothing surprised him any more.

He didn't have anything to look forward to.

Then, to his delight and excitement, his station sergeant informed him that there had been a report from Albany Street. Young Cuthbertson had been found in the wolves' cage in Regents Park Zoo.

'What in Christ's name was he doing there?' cried Superintendent Starkweather. 'Had he been drinking?'

'Not drunk, sir, apparently. Wouldn't say what his intention was. I suspect it was a prank, sir,' said the Sergeant intelligently.

'Bring me his file.'

'Yes, sir.'

The Superintendent read through the file of Police Constable Cuthbert Cuthbertson, five foot nine, medium build, and saw that he had the makings of an excellent copper. He had arrested hundreds of people, he was punctual, and he had scored top marks in everything at Hendon except Human Awareness. He leafed through the reports. His relief sergeant was impressed, the Dog Squad (with whom he had been on attachment) was impressed. Cuthbertson, it seemed, was a prodigy of policing. Why, then, this extraordinary aberration?

Superintendent Starkweather turned suspiciously to his medical history. Spitting blood? No. Recurring headaches? No. Nervous disease? No. Fits? No. Phobias? No. Dentures? No. Smoking and alcohol? Daily consumption zero.

As a last resort, he plucked out the personal form that recruits fill in themselves, only to discover that Police Con-

66

stable Cuthbertson's leisure interests encompassed 'Reading and Sport'. Reading, uh? That wasn't always a good sign. But Superintendent Starkweather knew he was clutching at straws.

A thought came to him. He buzzed the Sergeant.

'Was there anyone with Cuthbertson when he was detained at Albany Street?'

Rustling of papers.

'Yes, sir. I'm just typing up the details of the incident for you now. Bit of a problem with the ribbon, sir. No one seems to know the whereabouts of a replacement for the Olivetti Wordy Wonder Mark Three.'

'Lucky you never wanted to be a detective, Sergeant.'

'Yes, sir.'

'Get on with it.'

'Yes, sir. There was a young lady with him, apparently, sir. A Miss Arundell. Twenty-three, um, let's see, yes, lives in Eaton Terrace SW1.'

'Girlfriend?'

'Course not, sir. I'm married.'

'Not you, you idiot. Constable Cuthbertson.'

'Oh I see, sir. I don't know, sir.'

Superintendent Starkweather's mind sifted through the myriad aspects of this conundrum. The constable's motives, of course, must be ascertained immediately, then it could be decided what course of action must be taken. The blighter had broken and entered, it seemed, and trespassed, but there had been no theft. Had he intended to take something? And if so, what?

He had broken the Disciplinary Code, of course, but Super-intendent Starkweather was loth to lose the young man. He showed promise. There had been that dreadful tragedy with his brother, and his father had been on the force. A nice man, Cecil Cuthbertson, a nice man and a great Grand Master. He and Starkweather had broken the Frotteur case together.

However, as Superintendent Starkweather was only too aware, any decision he made would weigh on the perspective of the other young constables, and God knew they couldn't go about breaking into the cages of wild animals when the fancy took 'em.

Police Constable Cuthbert Cuthbertson, meanwhile, was becoming aware of one or two facts in his suddenly rather eventful life. First, it had been naive to hope that one could be a witch and a policeman at the same time. Second, he was falling in love with Rosaleen Arundell and would have to marry her as soon as possible if his life was going to hold any meaning. In the event that this project was undermined by lack of reciprocation he planned to implement what he had learned in Investigation Technique at Hendon – that if the same idea is repeated ceaselessly to a human being he or she tends, in the end, to agree with it. Cuthbert Cuthbertson planned to wear his intended down with subtle psychological warfare.

He arrived for the early turn at 6 am and was told to report to the Super immediately.

Superintendent Starkweather's office gave the impression that a burglary had just been committed and the police hadn't arrived yet. Every available surface was covered in shuddering dunes of paper, old coffee cups, old bits of Chinese takeaway, books about criminal law, a copy of the 1981 Scarman report and, for some inexplicable reason, an ancient edition of the *Blue Peter* annual.

PC Cuthbertson had a *Blue Peter* badge at home. He had received it when he sent three thousand pairs of old socks to their Land Rover for Ethiopia Appeal. His father had been furious at the time, because twenty-five pairs (black) had belonged to him and he hadn't finished with them.

The physical appearance of Superintendent Starkweather provided a startling contrast to the disarray in which he sat. He had never been known to appear in shirt sleeves, even in midsummer, and his uniform was a model of polished, ironed and gaberdine perfection. His grey hair had been smoothed and smacked into place by a pair of tortoiseshell hair brushes with his initials on them.

Hidden behind a fawn-coloured wallet folder on which the name of Cuthbert Cuthbertson was marked, Starkweather remained silent and immobile. Constable Cuthbertson wondered if he had gone to sleep. Then there was a jerk and the Superintendent's face appeared. He slapped the folder sadly on to his desk, slid a pair of Metropolitan Police issue

spectacles from the end of his nose and placed them on top
of it.

'Constable Cuthbertson.'

'Yes, sir.'

'Sit down.'

'Thank you, sir.'

'Constable Cuthbertson.'

'Yes, sir.'

'You're not at Oxford University, you know.'

'No, sir.'

'We're a laughing stock down at Albany Street. I hope you
appreciate that.'

'Yes, sir.'

'You are within six months of your final probationer's
examinations. You have been housed and trained at great
expense to the British public and now, at the final hour, you
show yourself to have criminal tendencies. Constable Cuthbertson, I think you owe us an explanation.'

Cuthbert was paralysed.

He could never admit to the occult nature of his project in
the wolf cage. At best it would destroy the little that remained
of his credibility as a police officer, at worst it would earn him
instant dismissal as someone linked with sexual sadism and
the ritual murder of children.

Superintendent Starkweather saw the young man's discom-
fiture and came to the only sane conclusion.

'Constable Cuthbertson.'

'Yes, sir.'

'Was it something to do with the young lady?'

Cuthbert breathed a sigh of relief. An escape route had
been provided as surely as if he had been handed a shovel
and told to tunnel his way to freedom.

'Yes, sir. In a way, sir.'

'Do go on.'

'Well, sir, it was a kind of dare.'

'And you wanted to impress her?'

'Yes, sir!' said Cuthbert with the confidence of a man who
has truth on his side.

'Constable Cuthbertson, I will not ask why the wolves' cage
and not the lions' den, because I'm not sure that I want to

know. However, I cannot emphasise the seriousness of this. A copper whose reports were not as good as yours would have been dismissed from the force immediately.'

'Yes, sir.'

'Nevertheless, you have scored top marks in most of your examinations and you have excellent reports from Sergeant Gacy. I see here that you would like to be a dog handler.'

'Yes, sir.'

'Rather ironic in the light of this current incident, don't you think?'

'Yes, sir. But I do like animals, sir.'

The Superintendent leaned back into his leather swivel chair, glanced up at the ceiling and then at the unhappy guardian of the Queen's peace sitting, helmet on lap, in front of him.

'I do not know, at this stage, how far the zoo wants to take this thing, and the proper authorities will have to be informed, but until I have had time to fully investigate this unhappy incident and discuss it with the Assistant District Commissioner I am putting you on report. Both the Sergeant and Inspector on your relief will write me daily records of your behaviour which will go on your file. If you have a flake of dust on your buttons, Cuthbertson, you will be dismissed from the force without further ado. Do you understand?'

'Yes, sir.'

'Whatever happens in your future these reports will remain on your file, as will the full details of this ridiculous action. They will, I have to inform you, seriously impede your progress, both in relation to your chances of promotion and with regard to transfer to the Dog Section. You have done yourself more damage than I can describe; however, I personally will not recommend your dismissal at this stage. The ADC may not agree with me, of course. He may think you are a felon, Cuthbertson, rather than a fool. You may go.'

CHAPTER NINE

The Vernal Equinox was drawing near. Soon the nights and days would be of equal length, winter would surrender, the icy winds would die and Eostra, Goddess of Spring, would be honoured. It was a time for optimism. Or should have been.

Sheenah had made herself another Protection Spell. Using double the ingredients, she charged it with the most powerful invocation she knew and hung it over the discoloured mark where the old one had been. Underneath she pinned a Lorica, written on recycled parchment and consecrated in the name of Isis, a goddess particularly skilled in the vanquishing of evil portents. She should have felt safe.

Nevertheless, every time she went into her garden she was reminded of the death of the robin, and a sense of loss breathed coldly upon her. As if to emphasise this, the bird table had been taken over by a gang of starlings. The result was that the small, attractive finches had disappeared and Sheenah was regularly faced with the gaping beaks of squawking oiks.

Vistas like this symbolised dissolution and shook her faith in the essential munificence of creation. Sheenah was determined, however, that no hint of despondency should break through her professional carapace. Her teaching skills, she knew, relied on the projection of her personality and this evening spells for love and happiness were scheduled. She owed it to her students to create an atmosphere that was conducive to the magical enhancement of these omnipotent qualities.

So, conscientiously suppressing deep feelings of agitation and disquiet, she enlivened her temple with the ambience of Eostra by decorating it with daffodils (bought from Simon in the organic fruit shop) and snowdrops (grown by herself in her garden). She made a garland of snowdrops for her neck and slipped into the copper cape that Liberace had given her when he had visited London in the Fifties. Copper, ruled by Venus, was known to initiate healing through self-love. Then she sprayed Paloma Picasso scent in the air and stood underneath the cloud as beadlets of scent dropped on to her shoulders.

These ministrations, invigorated by the drinking of dandelion wine from a ceremonial goblet, enabled her to display outward signs of confidence and optimism which she managed, somehow, to retain when Rosaleen and Cuthbert outlined the details of their catastrophe.

Sheenah was secretly appalled. There was not only Cuthbert's future to consider, but if the facts leaked into Wiccan circles she would become a laughing stock during this sensitive time, the lead-up to the election. Queen of the Witches was a position that required a dignified mien, a sense of responsibility and an unsullied image as well as the love and trust of witches around the country. These were the things that the Coven of Covens considered when tendering their votes. Sheenah's reputation was the symbol of her life-time achievement, and now it seemed in danger of being destroyed.

There had never been an episode like this before. Even her maddest novices had managed to locate wolf's hair, without attracting attention. She assumed they used their common sense and bought it in Merlin's shop. Steve had acquired some – from a friend, he said, and would not divulge any more. She did not know about Melinda, because she had not appeared this evening. The High Priestess felt a little anxious about the girl's absence. Unhealthy and thin though she was, she had seemed to enjoy the classes. Sheenah suspected she needed the company. A powerful premonition told her to ring Melinda at the next available opportunity.

Betraying no intimation of these stressful evaluations, she gave everybody a goblet of dandelion wine, sharpened with a measure of her best Cognac. Three thirsty throats gulped it down and she poured another round.

'Despite your misfortunes,' she said, smiling brightly, 'you managed to collect the wolf's hair, and its powers will be increased by these tribulations. Your Protection Spell will make you fireproof, bullet proof, bomb proof and' – she sipped her wine – 'fool proof. Fate will champion your every choice.

'You will be pleased to know that you are on the way to becoming true and great witches. Furthermore, today I am going to teach you spells of love and happiness. These will reinforce the powers of protection, attract good energy and bring joy and comfort into your lives.'

Rosaleen wondered if Andrew Grateman counted as good energy.

They all accepted another goblet of wine and, with a sibilant swish of her copper mantle, Sheenah led them in a hokey-cokey line to the kitchen where they sat in wooden chairs around the table and watched her demonstrate the making of a Love Philtre.

Taking down small brown bottles from various shelves, she poured concentrates of myrtle, rose, passion flower, motherwort and vervain into a Magi-Mix. To this she added mashed cumin seeds and blended in oils of strawberry and jasmine. 'A couple of tips,' she said. 'Not too much vervain because it smells, and never put primrose into a love potion. It only encourages wantonness.' Then she poured the mixture into glass vials with cork tops and handed them around. On each one there was a label saying 'Charged in the name of Aphrodite, Goddess of Love', and a dotted line for their name.

'Finally,' she said. 'For your homework I want you to ensure the success of this spell by finding a rose quartz crystal. Quartz, as witches know, have pienzo-electric qualities that link with the earth's currents. Different stones have different qualities, but we use the pink to attract love into our lives. When you have found one that feels right for you, wrap it in a white cloth and charge it by holding it and asking the Goddess to bring you an admirer who is correct for you and for the good of all.'

When they had gone Sheenah rang Melinda's number. She lived in the unfashionable end of Ladbroke Grove, and as Sheenah listened to the bell ringing into the unknown room she could imagine a flat in which the sound of the Westway could be heard. The lighting would be shadeless and there would be old editions of *Here's Health* and *The Vegan* lying around on tables whose supports were made of bricks. After some time (she nearly put the telephone down) a man's voice answered. It sounded almost as depressed as Melinda.

'Hullo?'

'Oh, hullo. This is Sheenah. I'm a friend of Melinda's and I was expecting to see her tonight. She didn't turn up and I wondered if she was all right.'

There was a long pause.

'Who did you say you were?'

'My name is Sheenah.'

'Oh, yeah. She mentioned you once or twice.'

The man spoke so slowly and so faintly it was difficult to hear what he was saying.

'I'm afraid I have some very bad news, Sheenah. Melinda, er, died.'

Sheenah felt her stomach fall.

'Died? When?'

'The police think it was last night, but she was found this morning. I'm her brother, Terry.'

'Oh, dear. I'm so sorry. Do they know what it was?'

'Yeah. They think it was malnutrition but there's gonna be an autopsy.'

'Malnutrition?'

'Yeah. That stupid diet. We were always on at her. Rabbit food and seeds. That's all she ate. She was always getting colds.'

There did not seem anything more to say. A young woman was dead. She had killed herself slowly and surely whilst under the impression that she was improving herself and her life.

The shock of Melinda's death transmuted into guilt and misery. Sheenah felt responsible. She had noticed how thin Melinda was. She should have done something about it. Cooked her a meal. Made her eat. Anything.

The gloom of presentiment intensified. The robin. The disappearance of the Protection Spell. Cuthbert. The death of Melinda. Either this series of sad incidents were the karmic repercussions of crimes committed in ignorance or they were the emanations of directed malevolence. Sheenah lay awake, her mind pitilessly harangued by a committee of inner voices.

74

Each shouted a different nightmarish theory, but about one thing they were all agreed. Myra was back in Sheenah's life, and with Myra came the degenerate forces of magical malpractice. The repulsion that Sheenah had felt when Harold had fallen in love with this woman all those years ago had naturally dissolved, but the memory of Myra's evil potential had not. Now, with twenty more years of experience and knowledge, Myra would surely use every technique at her disposal to remove opponents. She intended to defeat Sheenah and Sheenah knew for certain now that the competition to elect the Queen of the Witches was not to be a simple matter of counting votes.

The following Monday, Superintendent Starkweather arrived at the station to find a copy of the *News of the World* on his desk. There was a yellow sticker from Sergeant Gacy. 'I thought you ought to see this, sir,' it said.

At first Superintendent Starkweather was under the impression that officer Gacy was drawing his attention to a Miss Sharon Scoggins and her 'fun fur' bikini, but to the left of this item was a headline which he did not need his Metropolitan Police issue spectacles to read.

CULT LURES COPPERS
We Expose A Terrifying Trend That Puts The Security Of Our Nation at Risk!!!!

A bizarre incident at London Zoo has lead to allegations that British coppers are practising the evil art of witchcraft.

PC Cuthbert Cuthbertson, 21, was arrested last week after being found in the wolves' cage at Regents Park Zoo.

He told superiors at Shepherd's Bush police station that the break-in was a dare.

BUT WE AT THE *NEWS OF THE WORLD* KNOW BETTER!!!!

Informed sources in occult circles have told us that wolf's hair is required by witches to make their sordid spells and

**that more and more of Britain's policemen are being lured
by devil-worship and black magic.**

**'You just can't tell,' says the insider. 'By day they are helping
old ladies across the road and by night they are dancing naked
around bonfires and drinking bat blood.'**

That afternoon Police Constable Cuthbert Cuthbertson was
dismissed from Her Majesty's police force pending the possibility of further action by the Director of Public Prosecu-
tions.

CHAPTER TEN

Rosaleen conducted a meticulous search for the rose quartz crystal required by Sheenah's magic love spell. Most of the shops that she went to, the ones selling Indian jewellery, batik and incense holders, stocked minute pink pebbles that she didn't think would be powerful enough for her particular requirement. So, on a quest for a larger formation possessed of the force required to counteract months of involuntary celibacy, she went to see Merlin. His shop was empty and he was talking on a Bakelite telephone which he had customised with gold stick-on stars and Day-glo disco shapes.

'Yes,' he was saying. 'I know, darling. I told him he shouldn't have stayed the night. It only causes complications, frankly. He's been dating Gary for yonks . . . yes . . . yes . . . Well, now he's so paranoid he's started to insult himself so he knows what everybody is saying about him . . . I know, I know . . .'

He saw Rosaleen and signalled with a wave.

'Got to go. Customer. Kiss, kiss.'

'Hullo,' said Rosaleen.

'Hullo!' he exclaimed. 'How on earth are you? Enjoying Sheenah's classes?'

'Up to a point,' she said. 'You know we had a problem getting the wolf's hair?'

'Noooo.'

Merlin leaned forward on his stool wearing the expression of a person who usually knows all the information there is to know and can't believe he's finally about to hear some that he doesn't.

'Cuthbert and I went to the zoo and got caught in the wolves' cage. Well, Cuthbert did. He's in serious trouble.'

'Wolf's hair? Oh,' said Merlin. 'For the Protection Spell, I suppose. But you're silly boobies, you know. I have piles of it. I get it from my friend Gordon. He works at Whipsnade. I'm surprised Sheenah didn't tell you.'

'I think she wanted us to prove that we had some gumption. A kind of test or something.'

'Oh dear, oh lor, and it backfired. Mind you, taking a policeman into the class was asking for trouble if you ask me.'

'His father was a Freemason.'

'Anyway,' said Merlin, whose concentration span was limited to three minutes for each conversational topic that interested him, 'what can I do for you?'

'I need some rose crystal.'

'Oh yes?' Merlin's eyes twinkled in eurhythmic harmony. He knew of Sheenah's Love Spell. It was one of her most effective. 'I think I have just the thing you need, darling.'

He disappeared into a cavern at the back of his shop and after much stamping about and rustling reappeared with cobwebs wound into his beard and an antique trunk whose leather and brass, despite a light coating of dust, were in very good condition. He unlocked it and the lid sprang up to reveal a shelf on which there were hundreds of crystals and stones. They had been arranged in groups of complementary colours. The gold topaz and carnelians lay together, the green malachite and tourmalines were side by side, the blue moonstones and amethysts were in pairs.

'My jewels,' he said, pausing for a moment to stare upon this shingle of mineralogical marvels and reflect upon their exquisite tonal harmonies.

Then, slowly, he removed the top shelf to reveal the compartment underneath and there, glittering on a bed of sea salt, was a roseate rock of enormous proportions.

'Beautiful, isn't it?' he said fondly.

'Yes,' agreed Rosaleen, transfixed by the stone's flickering lights and comforting pink glow.

'It is the best and finest rose quartz I have ever seen. I've had it for ages and I've never wanted to sell it, but, Rosaleen, I somehow feel it is right for you. I have to warn you, though, it is very, very potent. It will need much tending and caring.

These things have a lot of energy. It was given to me by one of the Daughters of Branwen. It had been in her family since the seventeenth century.'

'Goodness,' said Rosaleen politely.

'Yes.' Merlin continued to look at it lovingly. 'This is no ordinary crystal.'

'How much?' she asked the persuasive bard.

'Seventy-five quid.'

'Credit card?'

'Of course, darling.'

Rosaleen handed over her card and Merlin wrapped the huge rock in white muslin. Then, with great difficulty, she manhandled it to her car where, placed on the back seat, its weight caused the front wheels to lift off the ground.

Twenty-five minutes after Rosaleen had staggered out, Merlin's telephone rang.

'Herne's teeth!' swore Sheenah. 'It's easier contacting the dead than it is getting through to you. You've been engaged for hours.'

'Sorry, darling.' Merlin leaned over to his Sony Discman and turned the Pet Shop Boys down. 'I've just had one of your students in here.'

'Don't talk to me about my students,' said Sheenah in a strangled voice. 'They're nothing but trouble this year.'

'Oh? Well, that little Rosaleen bought the rose quartz for her Love Spell.'

There was silence at the other end of the line.

'Hullo?' said Merlin. 'Are you still there?'

Another pause.

'Not that big one you got from the Daughter of Branwen?'

'Yes.'

'Oh, Merlin!' Sheenah was exasperated. 'How could you be so irresponsible? That stone was found in a sacred burial sight. It's supposed to be used for quelling riots and stopping wars. It's very powerful. Too powerful for Rosaleen. You might as well have given her an Uzi. She doesn't know what she's doing – she's a faery in a glen not bloody Aleisteir Crowley. Anything could happen . . .'

Merlin was taken aback. This turbulent manner was unlike Sheenah. Despite her Arian sun she was usually calm and optimistic.

'Is everything all right?' he said in an attempt to open out the conversation.

'No, it is not.'

'Rosaleen told me about PC Cuthbertson,' he said soothingly.

A loud sigh echoed down the line. 'I thought you read the *News of the World*,' she said.

'I do usually. Why?'

'There was an article about Cuthbert breaking into the wolves' cage. In the den of the Dagda I don't know how they found out. Anyway, now the poor boy's been sacked from the police force and there's a possibility of further action.'

This was serious. Merlin understood why Sheenah was uncharacteristically discordant.

'I don't know what to do. If they prosecute Cuthbert, they might decide to prosecute me – for inciting or accessorising or something. Should I resign from the election? Will the Coven of Covens find out?'

'There's no reason why the Coven of Covens should find out,' said Merlin, thinking fast. 'Your name wasn't in the article, was it?'

'No.'

'And as long as the cop keeps his mouth shut . . .'

'Do you think I should tell the Coven of Covens anyway?' asked Sheenah.

Merlin considered this for a couple of minutes, rubbing lemon-scented hand cream into his fingers and cradling the speaker between his neck and ear.

'No,' he concluded. 'I don't think that would be an astute move. You haven't done anything wrong so there's no reason why you should risk your position in the hustings over a hypothetical political possibility. In fact, I think you should adhere to the ancient laws of the Craft and counteract the negative with positive action. Send out your manifesto. Start enlisting support. Things like that.'

Sheenah muttered something about knowing how Persephone felt when Hades grabbed her and forced her to live in the Underworld, but Merlin pretended he had not heard.

'I mean,' he continued, 'we know Wales and West London will vote for you, but that's only two. Myra can rely on the Daughters of Calatin. If Angerboda announces a definite affiliation, then Sheffield and Carlisle will probably follow because they always take Angerboda's lead. Like bloody sheep. That leaves you with seven floating voters. Thor's Hammer are all friends of mine, so that's six.

'It's a matter of persuading those six to vote for you rather than Myra. They'll want to know what your basic policies are and where you stand on the issues – nudity, sex magick, nuclear power, the usual. I'll formulate a campaign strategy this week.'

'I wish I'd never gone up for this wretched thing now.'

'Nonsense! Granny Maldwyn would be proud of you. You've worked your whole life for this and you're the most suitable person to do the job. It's not like you to let a little bad luck get you down.'

'That's just it,' she said. 'I'm not sure it is just a little bad luck. I feel the Powers of Darkness pressing themselves upon me.'

'Don't be so silly.'

Thinking that the bedroom was the most appropriate place for a Magic Love Temple, Rosaleen placed the rose quartz there on the floor in front of the fireplace.

As luck would have it, that night marked the onset of a full moon. She waited until midnight was approaching, then, lighting some pink candles for atmosphere, she knelt down. Closing her eyes, she visualised all the men in the world whom she liked and tapped her magic wand on the huge crystal. As the carriage clock on the mantelpiece struck the hour, she said, 'May the powers of the Goddess bring me a lover.' Then she picked up the love vial and took out the cork, intending to sprinkle a few drops of the potion over herself. Unfortunately her hand slipped and all the contents disappeared down the front of her nightdress. A pungency that was disturbing, but not unpleasant, clung to her body, and pervaded the room.

Never mind, she reflected. It will make the spell more effective.

The next morning her doorbell rang at nine o'clock.

She stumbled clumsily down the stairs.

'Hullo,' said Andrew Grateman.

The few seconds that were required for the neuro-transmissions to confirm that this voice did indeed belong to Andrew Grateman were followed by the observation that not only Andrew Grateman graced her doorstep. Behind him stood Police Constable Cuthbert Cuthbertson and behind Police Constable Cuthbert Cuthbertson stood Steve and Dig accompanied by a milling throng of men whom she had never seen before in her life.

'Can I come in?' inquired Andrew Grateman. 'It's getting rather crowded out here.'

Stupefied, Rosaleen allowed the whole multitude to file through.

'I've lost my job,' Cuthbert shouted over the scrum. 'And I want to marry you.'

'I haven't lost mine,' said Andrew Grateman, shooting him a look of venomous hatred.

'I wondered if you'd like to come down for breakfast,' said Dig.

'I thought we might go for a ride in Hyde Park,' said Steve. 'Since the sun is out.'

Rosaleen hadn't felt so disorientated since the craze at school for sniffing aerosol deodorant out of plastic carrier bags.

'I haven't got any clothes on,' she announced. 'Why don't you all help yourselves to coffee? I'll see you in a minute.'

She hurtled upstairs. The rose quartz seemed to be glowing with lambent cosmic energy and the bedroom was heavy with the smell of jasmine and strawberry.

Rosaleen stared wildly at her complexion in the dressing table mirror. 'I can't be that attractive,' she said aloud.

Downstairs, to Andrew Grateman's intense fury, the kitchen had taken on the atmosphere of a workingmen's club, aided, in particular, by Dig who was drinking beer and, having assembled an unsightly quintet, was playing cards. The only people who should play cards before 6 pm, in Andrew Grateman's opinion, were those whose Christian name was preceded by an American state. The other men were draped in various postures about the place, drinking tea and airing platitudinous pleasantries. Then somebody turned on Radio One.

'I've had enough of this!' Andrew Grateman was not one for queueing. He ran upstairs to Rosaleen's bedroom where he stubbed his toe on the rose quartz.

'Woops!' said Rosaleen, who was leaning closely into her reflection in order to coat her eyelashes with Glossy Glo To Go mascara.

'Christ, Rosaleen,' said Andrew, hopping up and down and holding his foot, 'what the fuck is that brick doing there and why does this room stink of rotting ice cream and what are all those men doing downstairs? Most of them are saying they want to marry you.'

'I don't know half of them,' she replied.

'What about that one who's a policeman?'

'Ex-policeman,' she pointed out. 'I know him, he's a friend. But I don't expect I'll marry him.'

'I should think not. He's got red hair. Anyway, you said you were going to join a convent when we split up.'

His brindled fringe fell into his eyes giving him a deceptively boyish look, and reminding her how much she loved him.

'I'm on the cover of *L'Uomo Vogue* this month,' he added.

'Are you? How clever,' she said.

'Do you want to have dinner tonight?'

'Okay.'

'I'll pick you up at eight.'

'Okay.'

'I have a Lotus now.'

'Do you? How lovely.'

'Yes. I really am very rich indeed.'

Some of the crowd downstairs turned out to be meter readers and estate agents, others wanted to know when she was available. Rosaleen managed to despatch them one by one until she was left with Steve, Dig and Cuthbert.

'Dig,' she said, 'things are frantic here. Why don't we speak later?'

'Orright.'

Rosaleen turned around to see Steve evaluating her with eyes that were confused rather than cold or calculating.

Then, suddenly, he grinned widely, laughed and walked, without saying anything, out of the open kitchen door. She heard the slow clap of his heels down the hall and the click of the front door as it closed behind him.

There was silence.

Cuthbert could not believe his luck.

He produced a Burgundy-coloured Ratner's box from his pocket.

'Will you marry me?' he said.

'Cuthbert,' she said gently, 'I can't.'

He slid down his chair, shoulders rounded. 'I suppose I'm not much of a catch with no job or nothing.'

'It's not that. You're a very nice catch,' she lied.

'Is there somebody else?'

'Well . . .'

'That poncey git with the fringe?'

'Well . . .'

'I knew it.'

'Things are complicated. Let's put it that way.'

'I'll die if I can't see you, Ros.'

'You will see me, Cuthbert. Anyway, more to the point, what about you? What are you going to do?'

'I dunno. I'll have to find somewhere to live. They've told me to gerrout of the section house. And after that? I dunno. I've never done anything 'cept policing.'

'What about something similar, bouncer or something?'

'Nah. I'm not old enough.'

'I think we should ask Sheenah to do you a reading as soon as possible.'

Rosaleen made Cuthbert some breakfast, which he ate staring adoringly at her. Forks full of kedgeree kept missing his mouth and disappearing into the nigrescent crevice between his collar and neck. Then, clasping an *Evening Standard* newspaper, Cuthbert left to find accommodation while Rosaleen repaired to Madame Fabrice's salon in order to have herself made physically alluring for the date with Andrew Grateman.

'Blimey,' said Andrew Grateman. 'Your hair's got big.'

'It's always been quite big.'

'No, it hasn't. Mine's bigger, if anything.'

He took her to the most expensive restaurant in London where they sat on a banquette next to Cliff Richard.

Cliff Richard asked her out.

'He must like big hair,' said Andrew Grateman, who was mystified by the transformation that had come over Rosaleen.

He had not been surprised when Rosaleen had become funny about him. He had seen the symptoms many times before, but, recalling the rumour that her father was insane, he attempted to extinguish the heat of her ardour by leaving the country as often as possible. Now, though, the plump blonde prone to panic attacks had become a woman with sang-froid. A woman, even, of promise. It wasn't just that she had discarded her customary SW1 arrangement of pearls and floral print frock in favour of crushed velvet with antique buttons, or the fact that she smelled extraordinary. She was holding herself with an air of optimistic expectation. She wasn't clutching on to life's offerings as if they were about to be snatched away from her.

He studied himself in the mirror that lined the wall behind Rosaleen's head. He looked marvellous. The slate-grey Jean-Paul Gaultier suit not only highlighted the blue of his eyes but it had been cut so miraculously that his slightly narrow shoulders were made to appear of a width more proportionate to his height. Indeed, the outfit managed to bless his stature with an uncanny sand-kicking strength. The bleached white cotton Kenzo shirt was a masterful combination, as was the cunning silk tie decorated with embroidered letters that, on closer inspection, turned out to be a poem by e e cummings. He fingered it affectionately and was glad he had not opted for the one with an Art Deco motif.

They laughed and he paid. Then he came back to her house and they made love on the floor in front of the pink crystal.

CHAPTER ELEVEN

A couple of days later, Dig invited Rosaleen to the pub on the corner of Eaton Terrace where there was a fat Australian and hundreds of pinstripe suits. He bought himself a pint of Ruddles County and a whisky chaser, and her a Campari and orange juice.

Rosaleen had never really seen the point of pubs. The smell was awful and she would rather have had a Campari and orange juice at home, safe from the risk of being interfered with by the inebriated and irrational. Still, somehow they constricted themselves into a corner so that not too many people were touching them and Dig looked attractive in jeans, waistcoat and his long velvet coat.

He told her he would like to have played for Ipswich Town but he had gone to art school instead. He was between jobs at the moment, waiting to hear about a couple of interviews he had been to at glossy magazines. He seemed shy until after the second pint of Ruddles.

They had more drinks and he rolled a tiny tight cigarette from the Old Holborn tobacco he kept in a carved silver tin. On the hand without the tattoo he wore a silver ring in the shape of a skull.

He winked as he handed the cigarette to her.

'What would you like to do?'

'You,' she admitted.

Without saying anything he rose to his feet, threw the rest of the Ruddles down his throat and tapped the glass down on the concentric stains that patterned the table. As the spume in the glass melted away, he took her hand and raised her out of her chair. Still silent, he wrapped her coat around her shoulders and, continuing to clutch her hand, led her out of the pub.

CHAPTER TWELVE

'You're a very nice landlady,' he said, sitting up, rolling another cigarette and drinking the whisky he had bought to bed with him.

'Thank you,' she replied.

CHAPTER THIRTEEN

Merlin the Magus believed in bringing a sense of drama to his lectures and, in this, he was aided by the short time he had spent working in the special effects department at Pinewood Studios.

A space had been cleared in front of the sofa in the temple and a lectern bearing a large brass raven had been erected. This was spotlit from above while the rest of the room remained dark.

Merlin, like any intelligent artiste, did not socialise before his performance.

They all sat on the sofa, Rosaleen, Cuthbert and Steve, Rosaleen in the middle. There was little conversation due to the fact that they were all in love with the wrong person. Cuthbert made a few offerings about the weather and programmes only he had seen on television, but Steve said nothing.

The sofa was not long, but it was quite deep. Consequently it was easy for Cuthbert to press his hot body against Rosaleen's. She, meanwhile, tried to shift away without being offensive and lean into Steve who remained motionless, black Levis stretched out in front of him, taking no notice of either of them.

Cuthbert smelled of Paco Rabanne.

Steve smelled of leather and axle grease.

Rosaleen smelled of Moroccan souks and exotic fruit salads, the olfactory legacy of the love potion spill.

And as the sofa undulated with torrid body language their scents mingled together in the ether above.

Sheenah swept into the room followed at a slower pace by Catty. She (witch not cat) was wearing a red robe with medieval- style sleeves. Her lips and nails were painted the same hue, and the latter had black crescent moons painted on to them.

'Good evening, everyone,' she said. 'And blessed be.'

'Blessed be,' said Cuthbert.

'It is traditional in our sixth session of Witchcraft One to look at the deities that Wiccans worship and, for this, we invite a very distinguished lecturer indeed. May I introduce Merlin, Magus, Bard, Druid, Seer and Friend.'

The spotlight over the lectern went out, a Gregorian chant emanated from a cassette player and clouds of dry ice started to fill the room. This was followed by the sound of several firecrackers and then, with a larger bang and a puff of purple smoke, the figure of Merlin the Magus, Bard, Druid, Seer and Friend materialised behind the brass raven.

In front of him he had placed a torch with green cellophane wrapped over it which cast an eerie glow on to his face.

He was wearing long, white Druidic robes on the edges of which he had personally embroidered the Ogham alphabet in purple silk. When he swivelled to turn the cassette player off it could be seen that his hood was also lined with purple silk.

In his left hand he held a censer, the size and shape of a cricket ball, in which incense was burning. With his right he picked up a wand which he waved about and, as he did so, glitter streamed from the end of it.

'Good evening, heathens,' he said. His voice was strangely effete. After all the banging and smoke, a booming baritone would, perhaps, have been more suitable. 'I have come to you tonight to reveal the secrets of the ancients, the unknown mysteries of the western tradition that have fascinated innumerable souls throughout the centuries.

'Witches,' he continued, 'as you know, take the Goddess as their divine inspiration. She is a triune diety who manifests herself as the three faces of the Miraculous Female – Maiden, Mother and Crone. Now, for some people in this world the idea that God is a woe-man is at best heresy, at worst clinically insane. But let me tell those monotheistic bovver boys known as Christians, homo sapiens arrived years ago. Only two thousand of those years have been witness to that popular sect propagated by Constantine the Great.

'Before the rise of Zeus and Osiris, Odin and Jesus, the culture of the Great Goddess had existed for thousands and thousands of years. She was worshipped by the ancient peoples of Ephesus and the peoples of Mersin, the peoples of Hacilar and Alalakk. As the cosmic creative source she is celebrated by the Colombians in the Song of the Kagada Indians, as the Goddess Vari in the Mangaian cosmogony of Polynesia and as Nut, the sky goddess who, in the Heliopolitan tradition, produced the Egg.

'And so she has many forms, our Goddess, the Queen of Heaven, Divine Feminine and Creatrix Of All. She is Kali with her garland of severed heads, she is Bagala who destroys all negative forms and she is Bhairavi whose breasts are smeared with blood.'

Merlin interrupted the thrust of this violent imagery by taking a dramatic gulp from a silver goblet that stood on his podium.

'Historically,' he continued, leaning over the stand and staring into the semidarkness where his small audience sat, silent and agog, 'the cult of the Great Goddess is the basis of civilisation. I myself, who adhere to the Arthurian legend, have learned my skills from the Lady of the Lake, Viviane, or She Who Lives.

'It is not odd to worship a Goddess. You may think it is, but it is not. And for witches it is natural so to do, for theirs is a belief that attunes with the changing of the seasons and sits at the feet of the greatest goddess of all. And we all know who that is, don't we?'

He stared inquiringly at the sofa.

Silence.

'Mother Nature, of course! Mother Nature herself. And what of God? you may ask. Where is he? Well, we have a God, for witches believe in balance. He is awesome power, close friend and inner guide. He is Cernunnos, the Horned One, the deity of Celtic and Saxon traditions, and He is an essential complement and encouragement to She.'

Rosaleen glanced at Steve and wished He would be more of a complement and encouragement to Her.

Merlin concluded his lecture with an indoor firework which he had made himself and which flashed flames of red and green for some minutes after the spotlight had been switched off and the room immersed in darkness.

Rosaleen, Cuthbert and Sheenah clapped enthusiastically.

Steve looked distressed and uncomfortable.

'Lights please, Cuthbert,' ordered Sheenah. 'Tissane or wine anyone?'

Steve muttered that he was sorry but he had to be somewhere and he was late. Jangling his car keys he took long, graceful strides towards the door.

Rosaleen wondered why Steve always seemed to be running away, and whether these compulsive retreats had anything to do with her. She had never met anyone so handsome or so peculiar. It was an enervating combination and, provoked by it into irrational passion, she made an implausible excuse and ran into the night hoping to catch him in the street. But he had erased himself with the skill of one who is practised in the art of painless transience.

As Rosaleen had stared after the ebbing figure of Steve, so Cuthbert stared after Rosaleen. Seeing the look of doglike longing on his face, aware of her implicit role in the radical reorientation of his life, and keen to support him in the new direction that had been enforced upon him, Sheenah readily agreed to give him a reading.

She led him into an alcove that was partitioned off by a large black screen. There was a table with a tasselled cloth, two Windsor chairs and a framed press cutting from *Psychic News* which detailed her successes in the field of precognition.

'Now, Cuthbert,' she said, 'let's look into the crystal ball and see what your future holds.'

Cuthbert gazed intently into the clear orb that rested on a silver stand in the middle of the table. He saw nothing. Sheenah, presented with the features of Cuthbert staring intently into her ball, also saw nothing except the worried expression on his face distorted by the flection of the light.

But the crystal had never failed her and she continued to stare into it patiently, silently invoking the magic powers of the Goddess Isis as she did so. At last, as though through a mist, the images started to appear. She saw a disembodied hand lean forward and give a lozenge to a giraffe. Then she saw the same hand lift up a limp greyhound and put him in the back of a blue van.

'Have you ever thought of working with animals?' she asked him.

'I wanted to be a dog handler in the force,' he said, surprised and pleased at his hierophant's uncanny perceptions. 'And I like snakes.'

'Well, the ball tells us that there will be animals in your life,' she said, peering into the mystical depths. Then: 'I see you with them. You are smiling and very happy.'

'Great,' he said. 'Er . . .'

'Yes?'

She knew what he was going to say. She did not have to be clairvoyant to guess. One just had to have been born with the average quotient of common sense and a little power of recall. They all said it in the end.

'Er . . . What about the, er, opposite sex?'

Sheenah's sage-woman intuition, honed by years of work in this field, told her that former PC Cuthbertson's love life was not going to unfurl in quite the way he envisaged. She looked into the ball, but she already knew the answer.

'I see a young girl in the country. She is feeding ducks.'

'Do you recognise her?' said Cuthbert, inclining forward so that his nose pressed into the crystal ball and his breath steamed up the glass. 'I can't see her,' he muttered, squinting with ghastly intensity into the glassy sphere. 'What's she look like?'

'I'm afraid you won't see anything until you're a little more spiritually developed,' said Sheenah, pushing his face gently away. 'I don't recognise her, I'm afraid, but she looks very nice.'

'Blonde?'

'No. Mouse as far as I can make out.'

'Oh,' said Cuthbert, his face falling.

'I see great joy and satisfaction for you,' said Sheenah. 'I see you following the path that is correct for you. The Goddess gives us all we need, Cuthbert. Everything always works out for the best even if it is not necessarily what we had planned for ourselves.'

'I suppose so,' said Cuthbert. 'But I wish it had been Ros.'

He went home.

Merlin reappeared, having changed out of his Druidic robes, which were a little itchy, and into a comfortable tracksuit of pale mauve.

'They've all gone,' said Sheenah.

'Good,' said Merlin, 'because I need to chat to you in private.'

'Wine?'

'Yes, please,' said Merlin, who needed an anaesthetic. The evening had presented an unexpected shock which he was now going to have to communicate to Sheenah.

Sheenah lit some white candles for peace and they slumped into the sofa with their drinks. Somewhere above them there was the sound of loud footsteps clumping across the floor.

'Catty,' explained Sheenah.

'Right,' said Merlin. 'Sounds like an unwanted elemental.'

'Yes,' agreed Sheenah.

'And talking of unwanted elementals, darling . . .'

'Yes?' said Sheenah, who assumed Merlin was about to divulge some of the interesting gossip that he heard whilst talking on the telephone all day in his shop.

'How much do you know about your acolytes?'

'They all sent the usual letters,' she said. 'As you know, I don't really mind too much as long as there is some semblance of sanity.'

'What about Steve?'

'What about him?'

Sheenah feigned nonchalance but her heart delivered a warning beat.

'Do you not recognise him?'

'He does seem vaguely familiar,' she admitted. 'I've thought that all along. I wondered if he'd been on television or something.'

'I've seen him before,' said Merlin. 'It was a long time ago and he couldn't have been more than twelve, but it's definitely the same boy. I'd know those eyes and that jaw line anywhere.'

'Well. Who is he?'

Merlin gulped at his wine and this time it was not for dramatic effect.

'Myra's son.'

Sheenah sank back and attempted to assimilate the implications of this extraordinary deceit. Her powers of deduction were undermined by disbelief, but one fact floated to the surface of her conscience.

'He's Harold's.'

'I'm afraid so.'

'No wonder he looks so bloody familiar.'

'Yes.'

'What is the offspring of Myra and Harold doing masquerading here? Anyway, I thought Myra had called the baby some Irish name.'

'She called him Cu Cuchulainn, but he changed it to Steve because he was teased at school.'

'I should think so. Fancy calling a child Cu Cuchulainn!'

'I suppose she sent him to spy on you, to find out what your plans are and then sabotage them.'

'Damn her eyes,' said Sheenah. 'I should have followed my instincts or done a reading or something. I never trusted him.'

'If he's told her everything, she has a lot of ammunition,' said Merlin. 'I bet she rang the newspapers about Cuthbert and it's only a matter of time before names are named. You'll be the victim of a smear campaign.'

'She's out to get me, Merlin.' Sheenah's eyes widened as the weight of her opponent's desire impressed itself upon her. 'She's determined to be Queen of the Witches. She's very powerful, you know. What Myra wants Myra gets.' She shuddered. 'It's so creepy, sending her son.'

Merlin nodded, looked at his nails for a second and said, 'I don't think we should tell the brute. This will give you a silent advantage as well as the chance of planting disinformation. Just make sure he discovers as little as possible.'

'I can't believe this of Harold's child,' said Sheenah. 'He was weak, Harold, but he wasn't malicious. He didn't have a nasty bone in his body. Lazy, yes. Anything for a quiet life, yes. Wicked, no.'

'Quite,' said Merlin. 'But remember who his mother is, and she brought him up.'

They spent the rest of the evening discussing Sheenah's campaign strategy. The six floating voters were going to have to be approached with diplomacy and skill. Merlin was nervous that Cambridge (the House of Phoebe) and Folkstone

94

(the Faeries) would endorse Myra merely because she was a celebrity. These covens were resolute in their belief that the profile of the Craft should be raised in order to popularise the Old Religion and make it a mainstream faith. East London (the Norns) were radical feminists so they could go either way. Ireland, North and South, were traditionalists, which was in Sheenah's favour, and finally Levanah, clan mother of the Dark Women of Knowledge in North London, taught comparative religion in a polytechnic and was thought to be a moderate.

'Levanah is rather fond of the altered states of shamanic perception,' said Merlin enigmatically.

'She's pissed, you mean.'

'Or something.'

They played with the idea of badges and speeches and open-top cars, but Merlin thought this would alienate more people than it attracted. This was not an Illinois primary. It was a contest that would rely on the building of relationships and the careful projection of Sheenah's image to a select elite in an effort to persuade people that she would make a more responsible and prescient stateswoman than Myra.

Despite the presence of one independent and an unknown Alexandrian, this was a two-party contest.

Finally, they decided that an attractive photograph should be taken and a campaign leaflet sent out outlining Sheenah's biography, her position on the important issues and her vision of the role of Queen of the Witches (and the Coven of Covens) as they prepared to lead the nation's pan-psychics and eco-spiritualists into the twenty-first century and the dawn of the new pagan aeon.

CHAPTER FOURTEEN

Cu Cuchulainn, grandson of the giant Dagda and son of Lugh the God of Light, was known for his supernatural skills, super-human strength and an artillery of weapons that included the venomous spear of King Conchobar (the monarch said to have died from fury upon hearing of the birth of Christ) and the gae bulga, a harpoon with retractable barbs that was cast from the toes and could not be withdrawn from the body.

Cuchulainn the Conqueror had hair that was three shades, multi-coloured moles on his face and feet that could clutch like the talons of a hawk. Known for becoming very hot when aroused, his battle cry turned him, according to the legend, 'into a wondrous and hitherto unknown being'. He quivered like a bulrush in mid-current, his muscles stood out in lumps as large as the clenched fist of a fighting man and one eye sunk so far into his face ' 'tis a question whether a wild heron could have got at it'. Furthermore, his lion's gnashings caused flakes of fire to stream from his mouth, his hair resembled a thorn bush and the geezer of blood that shot out of the top of his head instantly transmogrified into a smoky pall.

He had killed three champions by the time he was seven and was only killed himself when the Daughters of Calatin forced him to eat dog, which was one of his 'geasa'.

Being divine, Cuchulainn was blessed with nineteen 'dessa' (gifts), including the ability to leap like a salmon. He possessed supreme skill at the game of chess, sooth-saying, discernment and beauty.

It was these 'dessa' that Myra had in mind when she christened her dark baby after the invincible Hound of Ulster and she had done everything within her magical powers to ensure that he was so blessed.

96

By the time he was twelve, Myra had made both her name and her first million pounds. They moved to Clapham Common and she sent him to Westminster, where he changed his name to Steve and managed to conceal the fact that his mother was a witch. He was naturally withdrawn, but became more popular when he was sixteen, thanks to the precocious ownership of a leather jacket which was the envy of the school.

As he made more friends, he managed to escape from his mother. Quiet at the best of times, he never volunteered the personal information that she wanted to hear. As a result, she often had to resort to readings, divination and looking through his pockets to ascertain what he was up to.

Now, at the age of twenty-four and showing few of the unusual attributes of his courageous Irish namesake, he had become, she had to admit, something of a worry to her. Van driving, she felt, was an inadequate return for the £30,000 she had invested in his education, not to mention the expenses incurred during the three long years he had malingered at St Martin's School of Art. Van driving was something that even people who had been educated by the state could do. But there he was. A Libra. Ruled by the passivity and hedonism of Venus. This had been a mistake. She had carefully conceived him to be a Scorpio, like herself, blessed with resourcefulness and drive. But he had been premature, and she had landed herself with a son born under an air sign. An air-head.

The problem was he was devoid of ambition. He actually liked driving vans. Sometimes he drove them for pop stars. Sometimes he helped people move house. On the days when there was no van driving to be done, he fiddled about making furniture from things he found in skips. It was inexplicable to Myra. She could not understand why he was not bored, and she could not understand why he was not about to become chairman of a merchant bank. The Gods knew she had done enough magic on it.

He arrived for lunch in his van.

Bacchus' balls, Myra thought furiously as she stood at the window and watched him back his frightful charabanc into a parking space outside the house. And he could have gone to university!

He bought her a lampstand that he had welded out of the exhaust pipe of a Mini Cooper. Although it was shiny and

97

curved and had taken him three weeks to make, she could only show the barest enthusiasm for she wished that he wore a suit and bought her flowers from Pulbrooke and Gould like other sons whose mothers lived in huge houses around Clapham Common.

'Pallas Athene has made you a nice game pie, darling,' she trilled, holding his hand and swinging it.

'Thanks.'

'So what is news with Mummy's competitor, then?'

It had taken Myra some time to persuade her son to join Sheenah's evening class. Despite his deep-seated desire for peace unadulterated by confrontation he had stood firm against the relentless tirades and loud weeping.

Then she had placed a large portion of what she described as his 'inheritance' into his bank account. This financial security offered Steve the chance to make furniture, which he enjoyed, rather than drive the van, which had no heater. Weakened by the choice between fulfilling artistic vision or freezing to death, and swayed by the prospect of a life devoid of nagging and threats, he had reluctantly agreed to infiltrate the Temple of Isis.

They sat down to eat lunch at the dining room table whose fine walnut had been polished to a veneer that reflected their faces. Steve at one end amongst a forest of candlesticks and dancing bear-shaped salt cellars, Myra at the other. To her left, on a plate, rested a white roll that was a paragon of circularity, whorled pats of butter and a butter knife with a mother-of-pearl handle. To her right lay the *Financial Times* rolled into a neat column and, on top, the reading spectacles which she never wore in public.

She forked the game pie genteely into her mouth, regularly lifting her starched linen napkin to dab at invisible specks that might have landed on her enlipsticked mouth.

Pallas Athene, whose inter-course appearances were controlled by a gold bell activated by the pressure of Myra's foot under the table, slid around as silently as a combination of petite physique and heavy tureens allowed.

Steve drank mineral water from one of the eight carved crystal glasses in front of him and wished it was a pint.

Temperamentally unsuited to intelligence work, and not relishing his position as purveyor of secrets, he revealed only

98

the most anodyne details about the last session of Witchcraft 1, failing even to mention that the lecture had been delivered by Merlin, a Magus he was certain he had seen somewhere before.

His mother's interrogation was less exacting than usual. Her concentration had been temporarily diverted by her forthcoming television programme, and she was as keen to talk about this as she was to hear of the affairs of her competitor in Shepherd's Bush. So, to his relief, she failed to fire her customary volley of questions and instead delivered a monologue about *Myra's Magic*.

'The BBC are very enthusiastic,' she said in her honeyed public relations tone. 'They think that man with spiky hair who spends his life locking people in wardrobes will have to retire.'

'So what's it going to be like, then?'

She explained that it would be what television people refer to as a magazine programme – a mixture of magic tricks, chat show, interesting facts and singing.

'Who's going to do the singing?'

'Me.'

'Are you sure that's a good idea?'

'Of course it's a good idea, darling. Don't you have any faith in Mummy's voice?'

Steve flinched.

'Now,' she continued, as Athene gently positioned thimble-sized coffee cups in front of them. 'Mummy has a very small little favour to ask of her darling.'

'What?'

'I need to borrow Sheenah's Catty for a spell.'

'What kind of spell, Mother?'

'The kind of spell that will ensure your mother is voted in as Queen of the Witches,' she replied.

'Why do you need the cat?'

'Because, as you know, when performing magic to further one's career, it is necessary to have the fur of an animal. A good plan is to have something that favours Bast, and an even better one is to have something belonging to the competition.'

'It is not a good plan, Mother. That animal is very difficult and very big. It will be impossible to get out of the house. Can't you use something else?'

'I need the cat,' snapped Myra, lips paralysed into a hyphen. 'And if you loved me, you'd get it. It won't come to any harm.'

He sighed deeply. When was all this going to end?

Where was it going to end?

'I'll think about it.'

'Well, don't think about it for very long. Your inheritance might run out.'

He got up from the table. 'I hope you're remembering the law of the Craft,' he said, looking down at her. 'I hope you are bearing in mind that "as ye sow so shall ye reap".'

Myra, of course, was not bearing this in mind, for she had stepped away from the right-hand path many years before this particular sermon.

After Steve had gone she swanned into her black temple in order to prepare for the arrival of Sheenah's cat. This animal of Bast would provide the final leverage that she needed. Choronozon required the blood of an animal sacrifice to make his full appearance and to energise his infinite powers of vengeance. Myra knew that if she drank the blood of Sheenah's familiar the white witch would be incapacitated for ever.

Turning counter-clockwise, she pointed her sword to the points of the compass and called forth the respective Knaves of Hell: Satan from the South, Lucifer from the East, Belial from the North and Leviathan from the West. Then she shouted her conjuration of Insurance of Success.

'Oh Lords of Darkness . . . I do kneel before you as Mighty Spirits of Death and I do dedicate myself to your work. Grant me the power to bring down thunder and lightning here in Clapham, and grant me the success of all earthly things and all that I desire.'

Around her she felt the supportive masculine presences of Baphomet and Baal, Choronzon and Moloch. They sent forth a soft wind that blew around her Chapel of Perfidy and caused the pages of her open *Book of Shadows* to flutter. As the energy surged up her spine, she experienced an orgiastic delirium, a heat and trembling throughout her body, and she knew that her wish would be granted. The animal would be brought to her so she could perform the curse known as the Ultimate Destruction of the Enemy.

100

CHAPTER FIFTEEN

Cynicism was not one of Rosaleen Arundell's dominant characteristics. Protected by the privilege of wealth, she had led a sheltered life bereft of the cowboy plumbers, cruel monks and lying employers that inhabit most people's existences. Any distrust that might have developed as a result of the simple process of growing older was stalled by the events that developed as a result of becoming skilled in the art of love magic.

The wondrous rose quartz crystal continued to exert its profound influence.

Rosaleen Arundell's ardent admirers celebrated her night and day.

She couldn't put a foot wrong.

Men in Texas rang in the middle of the night, men in Australia rang at dawn. Finally, when the third answering machine fused, she engaged an unemployed friend to act as social secretary and to field unwanted calls from cranks, convertors and beggars. Ivy spent most of her working day with her ear pressed to the telephone as she pencilled messages and appointments into the A3 floral desk diary that necessity had forced Rosaleen to purchase.

Ivy, amazed by Rosaleen's sudden popularity, viewed her as someone on a roll in a casino. She did not believe that this inexplicable run of luck could last, so she scheduled excursions, dinners, parties and picnics, one after another, into a hectic roster whose object was to make the most of the invitations before they stopped as suddenly as they had erupted. There was not a minute, it seemed to Rosaleen, when she was not either dressing, arranging how she was going to dress or going out on a date.

The quality of these dates varied. There were many *à deux* dinners when Rosaleen didn't know what to say to the stranger in front of her and cowered behind an artichoke. The men did not notice. Rosaleen was venerated by courtly lovers of all sizes, shapes and tax brackets.

Her jewellery box with the twirling ballerina had to be replaced by a small trunk in which she stored the gifts of pearls, rubies, antique gold chains and things that arrived in Tiffany boxes. Her house exuded the heady odour of the orchids, lilies and roses that arrived every day in cellophane and in cardboard boxes.

She and Ivy arranged a complicated filing system as the magnitude of numbers began to oppress them. A lord would ring from Sutherland and Ivy would flick through the index cards to ascertain his exact identity. Under his name there would be a record, written by Rosaleen, outlining the location of previous encounters and the standard (out of ten) of his sense of humour. If the latter was low the unfortunate individual would be relegated to the 'M' file (Miles Too Boring Ever to Talk to Again). Sometimes a press cutting would be attached to the record and, if relevant, cross-references to page numbers in *Debrett's* (hereditary peers), *Spotlight* (actors) and the *Guinness Book of Hit Singles* (musicians).

Soon London's society sisterhood began to pay attention. There were secrets to be learned from Rosaleen Arundell. No one (they told each other) could be that plain and that beloved without having something useful to reveal. The legend circulated that Rosaleen Arundell was a sex maniac, a mistress, it was said, of the Topless Hand Shandy. This was soon refuted. Rosaleen did not have time to sleep with anyone. Whirling vortex of activity though she was, intimacy, oddly, was beyond her reach.

Terence Grey reappeared. He gave her a Cartier watch with diamonds set in the face, took her to the Ritz in his Daimler, wept and said he missed her. Rosaleen replied with a truthfulness uncursed by conceit that she thought she had an opening in August.

She went out a couple more times with Dig, but he had become thin, unpredictable and tired. It was very disappointing. If he hadn't been born with cheekbones he would have been demoted to the 'M' file. Once he fell asleep during the first course. His face dropped into a bowl of taramasalata and he would have suffocated had it not been for the presence of mind of a (delighted) waiter named George who threw him to the floor and gave him mouth-to-mouth resuscitation.

Cuthbert's cravings had not survived the transpontine move to Battersea, where he was working at the Dog's Home and had applied to join the RSPCA. She saw him at the Witchcraft 1 evening classes and, although he stared without discretion at her breasts, he managed to remain calm. Despite the furore of her social assignations, Rosaleen honoured her commitment to Sheenah's course, partly out of respect to the witch but more because she was still ineluctably drawn towards Steve. His insouciance combined with a way of holding people's attention by gazing with those indecipherable black eyes incited a desire that bubbled on the brink of hysteria. It seemed to Rosaleen that he was flirting.

Perhaps Steve was not as immune to the power of the rose quartz as he had at first appeared.

Sheenah, who took them through the Moon (with assorted auguries) and Reincarnation, grew more and more distracted. After every session she delivered histrionic warnings about the Daughter of Branwen's stone and begged Rosaleen to be careful. The quartz, she insisted, once belonged to the White Tornado of Tiverton.

'What,' Rosaleen unsurprisingly asked, 'was that?'

'I don't know exactly,' she was told, 'but he was a wizard and he died of syphilis.'

On the day *Today* newspaper announced that Rosaleen was their 'Girl of the Year' Andrew Grateman's Lotus slid gracefully into Eaton Terrace.

'Have you got an appointment?' Ivy inquired, looking up from a schedule on which a rash of colour-coded dots had been placed.

'Don't be ridiculous,' said Andrew Grateman from behind his Ray Bans. 'Who are you?'

He couldn't understand why he was in the presence of this small, bossy and unfamiliar woman whose tight black curls gave her the appearance of a blackberry that had reached the end of the season without being picked.

'I am Miss Arundell's secretary,' replied Ivy with diva dignity.

'What does she need a secretary for?'

'Her engagements, of course. Miss Arundell is very busy. I've already got three luncheons pencilled in for next March.'

'Don't be funny,' said Andrew Grateman with genuine incredulity. 'No one has a social secretary in this day and age.'

'Miss Arundell does.'

He focussed his Ray Bans on her for a couple of intimidating seconds.

'I'll just wait for her, then,' he said and glided into the kitchen to make himself a cup of coffee with the Zen assurance of one who knows he is always welcome.

Rosaleen returned twenty minutes later. She had been having breakfast at Claridge's with an earl whose name (despite the index cards) she could never remember. She had peered hopefully at the crest embroidered over the breast pocket of his Turnbull and Asser shirt, but it had provided no clue to his identity. She knew that his name was the same as a coastal resort but was certain it was not Warbleswick.

Andrew Grateman's feet (in black Italian loafers) rested upon the pine kitchen table. By the side of them lay a box of 'Extra Mild' Silk Cut and a pocket of matches whose logo indicated that they were a complimentary gift from the Polo Lounge of the Beverly Hills Hotel.

'Really, Rosaleen,' he said, rising smoothly to a vertical position which enabled him to look down his nose, 'what is going on here? It's as if Harold Pinter had taken to writing West End farces.'

'You've got lunch with a judge,' Ivy interrupted. 'You had better change.'

'Fuck the judge,' said Andrew, 'Come out at once with me.'

Andrew Crateman's single-minded inflexibility had been responsible for the peaks to which his career had soared; contradiction was a waste of breath and, anyway, Rosaleen had had no experience in trying.

'All right,' she said.

Raising her eyes to the ceiling like a Renaissance madonna, Ivy scribbled furiously on her clipboard. After a lot of muttering, the judge was cancelled and Andrew drove Rosaleen (lying down because they were in his Lotus) to Kensington.

His six-storey house, with strawberry pink walls and pepper-mint green window sills, stood out in the white street like a knickerbocker glory.

He led her to the very top where, in a glass-roofed studio, books were arranged by the authors' countries of origin. His collection of Art Deco was displayed in highly polished steel cabinets. Grinning harlequins and archers wearing gold togas posed alongside women in chain-mail headresses whose bodies appeared to be moving against an unseen hurricane. The portion of the room not occupied by desk, computer and Oscars had a stripped wooden floor scattered with brightly coloured Kelim rugs.

'I'll make us a Sea Breeze,' he said.

Rosaleen sat on the ivory sofa. 'You look well,' she told him.

'Yes.' He touched the tan whose depth was due to weekends in Malibu, and whose lack of flakiness was due to regular applications of Kiehls moisturiser. 'I've been in California talking to Columbia about *Subhumanoid Sheila*. It'll be practi-cally impossible to make into a film since there is only one scene in it, but they hadn't noticed and I certainly didn't tell them.'

Then, suddenly, he pirouetted. 'Do you think these trousers are good?'

Andrew always chose traditional classics woven in unusual hues and, today, he had teamed a dusky orange chambray shirt with a tie whose Fornasetti suns smiled enigmatically from it. The black wool pleated trousers that had been acquired in Comme des Garçons fell deftly on to deep purple socks.

'Very nice,' said Rosaleen.

She couldn't help thinking, almost in spite of herself, of Steve in his leather jacket, Levis and worn cowboy boots.

'No one cuts like Comme,' he said. 'Shall we have Mozart's *Sinfonia Concertante* in E Flat Major?'

'Okay.'

He put the music on, gave her the drink and guided her towards his power shower where hard jets of water crashed in on the body from eight different directions.

Later, when Rosaleen's features had fallen back into their usual pre-coital design, the playwright lit a cigarette and stared for a second at the framed photograph that had been taken at the Broadway opening of *Late-Night Chopping*.

'So,' he said. 'Let's get married.'

Rosaleen gazed at the ceiling.

She felt as if she had been run over.

Here was the man with whom she had been obsessed for nearly three years. The man whom she dreamed about and woke up in the morning still thinking about, the man over whom she had nearly crashed her car because she was looking at the pavement to see if he was walking down it; the man whom she opened newspapers to read about and watched the television to see; the man for whom she had put on make-up and hung around in a late-night supermarket in Ladbroke Grove (where there were people with ratchet knives) because she knew he bought cranberry juice there. The man whom she had slimmed down for, taken up smoking for and consulted plastic surgeons for. The man who possessed that region of the mind over which there is no control.

The power of the rose quartz was beginning to frighten her.

But everything had changed. The temptations of freedom had introduced themselves. There were discoveries to be made and borders to cross. She was popular. She was loved. The shroud of loneliness no longer threatened. Desperation had dissolved. And so, for the first time, she questioned both the nature and the depth of the feelings she had imprisoned for so long.

'Um,' she said. 'That's very kind of you. Can I think about it?'

Andrew wondered if the Ramones concerts he had attended as a teenager had chosen this moment to have an adverse effect on his hearing. He swallowed as if to pop his ears.

'What?' he said. 'Think about it? *Think* about it? How extraordinary! Yes, I suppose so. But don't take too long, Rosaleen. I am rather in demand.'

'Yes, I know. I'm very complimented.'

'And fantastic at sex . . .'

'Indeed.'

'Four times, you might have noticed . . .'

'Yes.'

He stubbed out his cigarette, got out of bed and spent some minutes straightening the frame of his painting by Jean-Michel Basquiat.

He was quite silenced by surprise.

106

CHAPTER SIXTEEN

There were times when Dig wished he had not chosen to rent a flat quite so near the Algerian Embassy. The policemen stationed on guard outside it stood opposite his window and seemed to stare through it twenty-four hours a day. This unrelenting surveillance was effecting the quality of his life.

If the policemen had been issued with pairs of X-ray spectacles that enabled them to see through curtains that were drawn day and night, they would have observed that Dig's sitting room comprised rows of bodies that lay in front of a flickering television set underneath a cloud of marijuana smoke. These quiet figures, in jeans and sneakers, rarely moved, and if they did it was with leaden torpor and uncoordinated motor mechanism. Hands clasping at the walls, they would guide themselves blindly towards the fridge and lethargically pull out a can of beer.

Around the room were the curled and fissured symbols of narcotics culture – silver paper cross-hatched with brown streaks, scissors, black matches, spoons, glassine envelopes, scales, and dozens of packets of cigarettes whose lids had been torn to shreds.

Occasionally, very occasionally, somebody would speak:

'Uh, Dig, man?'

'Yeah, man?'

'Where d'ya put the stuff, man?'

'Uh, I dunno. It's in the bedroom, I think.'

'Right.'

Long pause.

'Ur, Dig, man.'

'Yeah, man.'

'Where's the bedroom, man?'

And:
'This is good shit, man.'
'How much d'ya pay for it?'
'Twenty a quarter.'
'Yeah. It's good shit, man.'
And:
'Roland, hand over that joint before I rip your fucking head off.'

Dig liked taking drugs a good deal more than flogging around the West End with his portfolio of magazine lay-outs attempting to persuade epicene art directors to employ him. He preferred smoking smack to standing about with neurotic photographers, and he thought his hands were put to better use making bongs from scooped-out grapefruits than cutting out bits of paper with a scalpel.

He had met the right man at a party and the right man's supply arrived at regular enough intervals to grant Dig a reputation for being one of the most reliable dealers in Chelsea. His profits were all spent on personal stimulation, but so what? He was having a good time. He couldn't understand why heroin had such a bad name.

He lit a small, tight, one-skinned joint made out of neat grass and put on a video of *Re-Animator*. Dig loved *Re-Animator*, and the more stoned he became the greater the film seemed until, by the end of the joint, *Re-Animator* was the B-movie equivalent of *Citizen Kane*. Or something like that.

Herbert West injected his luminous reagent into the neck of Dr Hill.

Dig leaned forward, silver tube in mouth, put his face over the curved tinfoil in front of him and sucked deeply on the sweet smoke that snaked up from it.

He felt well. Very well.

CHAPTER SEVENTEEN

Myra's television show was aired on Saturday evenings after the news and before a popular American series about a doctor who had turned into a detective halfway through his career. It starred a Las Vegas singer who had turned into an actor halfway through his. It was a prime-time position coveted by hundreds of light entertainers. Several suspicious individuals stood in the BBC bar and wondered who this Myra had slept with in order to earn such a slot, but the more generous argued that it was merely a sign of the corporation's confidence in its new star.

Myra was the consummate professional. She was never late for rehearsals, she read an autocue with natural skill, she was relaxed in front of the cameras and she was a lively interviewer. The only eructation that had occurred during the smooth flow of contractual negotiations was the row about her wardrobe allowance which, she was told, was more than the Director General earned in a year. She had retorted tartly (through her lawyer) that this must be the reason why his suits looked like board games.

Myra knew that fabulous glamour was the secret of screen success. She also knew that Chris, the lighting technician, was the most important member of the crew and quickly initiated a warm friendship with him. Consequently she never looked a day over thirty-nine.

The show was recorded in front of a 'live' audience which amused her. 'They couldn't very well be dead, could they?' she informed her producer with a simper. A worried man in a grey cardigan, Neil had recently been forced to transfer from a religious programme because whenever his name had been shouted across the studio floor, everybody did.

The first programme of Myra's series went like this:

As an instrumental signature tune of 'Saved', the Laverne Baker R&B classic, was played on glockenspiel, Myra appeared on top of some silver stairs and stood like a secular goddess of the Forties – arms splayed above head, one leg in front of the other, hips and cleavage jutting out as if about to go off somewhere by themselves.

The full glories of the first of three outfits were thus revealed.

Then, with subtle insinuations of silk and multicoloured ostrich feathers, transporting a smile that could melt tarmac, she walked slowly down the stairs singing her tune, 'I Used to Smoke, Drink, Smoke, Drink, Do the Hoochie Coochie', and sat on a gold chair with a red velvet cushion. By the side of this, there was a plainer seat (for her guest) and a table on which there was a pack of Tarot cards, a magic wand with a star on the end of it, a crystal ball and a vase of flowers.

She began with a card trick involving a member of the audience (camera close-ups of expressions of wonder and amazement when 'volunteer's' ace of spades was found inside an uncut water melon). After this, a Ufologist was interviewed. This was followed by a short film entitled *Myra's Miracles*, which featured a believe-it-or-not story about a ghost in a pub in Purley.

She concluded by singing one of her 'personal favourites', which she hoped, 'the audience will come to love as well.'

The Times noted that the regular alternation of Myra's dresses was a more mystifying visual illusion than her card trick. In general, though, the notices were favourable and, anyway, as Neil pointed out, it didn't matter what the critics said because no one took any notice of them.

Myra's Magic show stimulated the imagination of the nation. She received thousands of letters. Some were illegible, some were sinister, many were gratuitously inquisitive, but most were laudatory. To the surprise of market researchers she crossed over into the youth and gay markets, both of whom liked her because she was camp and therefore funny, although neither Myra nor her press officer was aware of this.

And so, as she knew she would be, as Choronzon and the Lords of Hell had decreed, Myra, Mistress of the Stars and

110

Mother of the South London Sisters of Diana, became a celebrity.

She was on the cover of the *Radio Times*. She could (and did) demand £7000 to open boutiques in Crawley. She was photographed everywhere she went. Fashion magazines asked her to model, publishing houses asked her to write books . . . well, not write them exactly, but read them and sign her name if she liked them. Coffee and shampoo companies asked her to be in their advertisements, designers sent samples. CBS asked her to make a single of 'Saved' and the popular press ran hundreds of articles about her love life, which they made up by superimposing pictures of her standing next to Nigel Havers and Ian McShane.

Myra granted no interviews, which succeeded in whipping the media into a frenzy of myth-making. Her PR told everyone that the Mistress of Magic was a shy person and terrified of being burgled, but Myra was aware that mystique bred longevity and she did not allow her ego to blind her to the fact that journalists were paid to pry. If they should discover any hint of her relationship with the Masters of Darkness, the damage would be irrevocable.

Although she refused to speak, she occasionally allowed a photographer (of her choice) to shoot some colour pictures for the middle-market magazines. They were read by the housewives and pensioners who comprised the main sector of her following. For these women she was an omniscient guru elevated by beauty and an ability to hear Messages from Beyond.

She also made carefully timed visits to hospital wards (particularly those in which there were children) and hosted a couple of well-publicised charity events so, despite her high-profile reticence, she was soon being called things like 'Myra! Woman of the People'.

The week after 'Saved' achieved the number one position in the hit parade and her video had appeared on *Top of the Pops*, her PR informed her that surveys were showing that she was more popular than the Princess of Wales.

CHAPTER EIGHTEEN

In the Celtic tradition that is so closely related to witchcraft, the Annual General Meeting of the Coven of Covens was always held on 21 June, the solstice known as Midsummer. Although this is not a greater Sabbat, imbued in pagan eyes with the import of Beltane or Samhain, it had become of significance to the thirteen members of the Coven of Covens because it was named in their constitution as the date when the delegates for Queen of the Witches were officially nominated. It was written in *The Very Moste Secrete Booke of Witchery* that the 'sovereigne of the Craft of the Wise' must step aside in order to allow the 'Very Moste Reverend Council of Elders also known as the Coven of Covens' to elect a replacement. A further clause revealed that 'any starre in the skye mighte be Queen' but that the candidate must be over eighteen, a third-degree initiate, live in the area represented by the Coven that nominated her and never have 'spilled the blood of any living swain'.

Although the rules of leadership outlined in the *Booke* decreed that Elders were allowed to vote for whomsoever they chose, in reality they took the list of candidates home with them, held long discussions with their own covens about the respective qualities of the nominees and voted in accordance with majority opinion.

Over the years there had been many moves to make this practice statutory by those who felt that a bill should force members of the Coven of Covens to represent the wider opinion of the Craft rather than, when it came down to it, their personal sensibilities. However, these motions were always thrown out by the majority who felt that freedom to express their opinion and judgement was the point of sitting on this hallowed committee. They did not want to become puppets, they said. Thus the democratic process could only go so far in this arena of enlightened ones.

All this, had been academic for the past twenty-five years because Angerboda, despite numerous attempts to oust her, had continued to be voted in year after year. She was a popular stateswoman with much experience, but her resilience and tenacity were still extraordinary. She could, most witches agreed, have gone on until she was eighty.

But now Angerboda wished to retire, and the Annual General Meeting of the Coven of Covens promised to be electric with tension because, in some ways, this was the first truly competitive election for many years.

The Sabbat was held in the parish hall in Chipping Cadbury, with the blessing of its broad-minded vicar. Angerboda opined that this was because he was Irish, a race famous for their libertarian attitude towards unorthodox psychic principals and who had murdered few witches even at the height of the Burning Times. The equanimity of the ecclesiast did not extend, however, to the lighting of a fire in his hall, so they had to be content with a cauldron full of symbolic red and yellow tissue paper, and candles whose positions had been inspected by the local fire department.

The room was decorated by Merlin, who spent three days balanced on top of a stepladder, pins in mouth, armed with a staple gun with which he affixed flowing cascades of brown, yellow and gold fabrics. Gold and yellow were the traditional colours of Midsummer. They represented the sun, and would be worn by all members of the Coven of Covens in keeping with a dress code that had been a tradition of the Annual General Meeting since 1903.

The Oak King and Holly King, twin sovereigns of folk lore, were represented by bunches of foliage arranged in wooden barrels. Chaplets had been made for the heads of Freya and Merlin who would represent the Maiden and God respectively. Merlin secretly wished that it could be the other way around but knew that worshippers of nature would not be influenced by this untraditional perspective. The rituals of the Coven of Covens were conventional, in terms of Wicca, in that they adhered to and upheld the polarity of sexual balancing.

113

The Elders started to gather on the steps of the hall at around 6 pm. The meeting did not begin until 7 pm but a photo-call had been agreed to at the request of the *Chipping Cadbury Inquirer*. Angerboda promoted a policy of *glasnost*, because in her view stealth and suppression stimulated imaginative rumours and wearisome propaganda. In general, though, the village was welcoming. The landlord of the local pub, where many of the dignitaries and occultists spent the night, mixed a commemorative cocktail which he called 'Mid-summer Mayhem'. Most local people were quite accustomed to the eccentricities of Angerboda and her friends and most of them, over the years, had been comforted by her rune-readings.

The Sun God, in philanthropic mood, bestowed a fine evening over Chipping Cadbury and a crowd gathered outside the parish hall to watch the arrival of the Coven of Covens.

The procession was always a splendid pageant, but this year, in honour of Angerboda's long and victorious reign, everybody had made a special effort.

From the distance they looked like a lemon and gold caterpillar squirming down the quiet country street, but close up each imperial individual was a vision of luxury and pomp. Burnished diadems sat on proudly held heads, fine-spun gold girdles wound around primrose-coloured robes, ochreous pantaloons were wittily slashed to reveal shards of crimson silk, floor-length habits were made from marigold paduasoy. Some headdresses were constructed from pussy willow and heather, others with whorled Celtic-style metalwork. Many carried the crooks of Osiris and the pipes of Pan, but there were also sistrums and swords, scimitars and cadaceuses.

Merlin looked incredible in an outfit inspired by Robin Hood that coordinated yellow hose and a brown velvet cloak with a stag's head embroidered in gold.

'Hello', 'Peace' and 'Blessed-Be' could be heard as a Sister of Morrighan hailed a Sheila na Gig from Sheffield and the Arch-Priestess from the Oracle of Queen Maeve greeted the Handmaiden of Hermés.

As the last rays shone down on the witches, oviates and mystics, the man from the *Inquirer* bent forward, looked into his viewfinder and told them all to smile. And smile they did,

114

for there was much to smile about at this grand and exciting convention.

There was also much to discuss.

The foremost conversational topic was Myra, leader of the Sisters of Diana, contender to Angerboda's throne, and media megastar.

'I think it's a disaster,' said Eirene of the House of Phoebe, as she took her position at the long council table. 'I've never liked Myra, but what can you do? All the witches around me in Cambridge can't talk about anyone else. She's so famous now. Everybody seems to love that programme of hers. I'm going to be under tremendous pressure to vote for her.'

'It's the same in Hackney,' sympathised Nepthys, leader of the Norns. 'Everyone is mad about her, but frankly I can't see what swanning around half-naked in ostrich feathers is going to do to enhance the image of the Craft. I'm trying to persuade my lot to vote for Sheenah. Her work with the Liberation League has been splendid and there is nothing self-aggrandising about her. I think she would make an excellent Queen.'

A minority knew Myra well and they were recognisable by their air of saturnine detachment. They knew that no Gorgon, no Argus, no lofty Gromer Somer Joure would stop Myra getting what she wanted and their souls shrank at the thought of one such as she becoming their spiritual leader. Levanah, leader of the Dark Women of Knowledge, was grim and taciturn. She had received a late-night visit from two of Myra's supporters in which it was intimated that her heavy drinking bouts were not a suitable pastime for one employed by the Greater London Education Authority. It was suggested that an informative letter might be sent to the relevant department unless the Dark Woman of Knowledge's vote was cast in a suitable direction.

Quiet, too, was Bridget of the Oracle of Queen Maeve, for she had accepted a generous offer to appear as a guest on Myra's show and talk about her forthcoming memoirs, *Which Witch is Which?*

'The problem is,' piped up Vesta of the Sheffield Sheila na Gigs, 'Sheenah is only known in London. If only she had cast her net a little wider . . .'

'She's known in Wales,' snarled the Daughter of Branwen. 'And let us not forget that she is an hereditary witch, whereas Myra is a husband-stealer.'

'I think,' boomed the rumbling Highland burr of Charles, High Priest and Liege of Thor's Hammer. 'I think that Myra is a lassie who has forgotten the wee Hermetic Law of Correspondence. She does not, as the leet greet William Blake put it, hold infinity in the palm of her hand nor see eternity in an hour.'

There was a short pause as this cryptic point was analysed for magickal and philosophical content.

'No,' observed Merlin from the opposite end of the table, 'though we feel eternity in half an hour if we have to watch that television show of hers.'

But everyone knew that Merlin was partisan.

Suddenly the sound of a flute filled the air and there came the rhythmic banging of a tambourine.

'Sssh!' hissed the Hermés Handmaiden. 'Here comes Angerboda.'

The Coven of Covens lapsed into a respectful silence and stood up as Angerboda walked slowly down the hall, much as a bride glides down an aisle. Tall and resplendent, she wore a gold vestment inspired by the Viking queens of her heritage. Around her chest was the embroidered silk sash worn by all Queens and, on her head, the triple-pointed crown. Under one arm she carried *The Very Moste Secrete Booke of Witchery*, a huge black tome around which there was a padlock the size of a baby's head. She was followed by Freya and Frigga who carried velvet cushions on which lay the Queen's athame and sceptre.

Angerboda took her place at the top of the long table which had been covered in a green cloth and beautified with a central motif of oak and holly leaves. At each place there was a glass of water, paper, pencil and a photocopied report of the previous year's AGM. Surveying the faces that, like sunflowers, had all turned towards her, she waved her hand with gentle (though royal) benificence and indicated that everyone could sit down.

The Folkstone Faery, who had been smoking a Benson and Hedges on the porch, scuttled in.

'Greetings,' said Angerboda, 'and Hail to the Goddess.'

'Hail to the Goddess,' chanted the Coven of Covens.

'*Honi Soit Qui Mal y Pense.*'

'*Honi Soit Qui Mal y Pense.*'

'Welcome to the annual general meeting of the Coven of Covens held this day, Thor's Day, ruled by Jupiter, exalted by Mars, and in the honour, as always, of the Goddess.'

Angerboda's opening speech was videoed by Taliesin, a friend of Merlin's who had started an occult home video business thanks to the generous sponsorship of a Japanese fashion magazine.

'As Queen of the Witches,' Angerboda said, 'I have seen much progress for the Craft, both in the public image that is presented by the press and in the very numbers that are joining us. As every year goes by more and more women are drawn to the gentle powers of our Earth Mother and Goddess; as every year goes by the congregations of the churches fall as more and more people choose alternative spiritual paths. The New Age has arrived, as we all knew it would, and, although individuality is the very essence of Wicca, we must do everything we can to present a united front, for this is and always has been the purpose of the Coven of Covens – to protect, to heal and to help.

'We may be Alexandrian, we may be Dianic, we may be Gardnerian. Whichever route we have decided to tread, we must never forget the Ancient Tradition from whence we came, the tradition that sees us as the wise woman of the village endowed with a Goddess-given talent which enables us to heal as well as offer spiritual solace. We are not the shape-changers and devil-worshippers of Isabel Gaudi's confessions. We are not hags in pointed hats. We are modern and liberated and we were involved with environmental issues many years before the launch of Greenpeace.'

Tumultuous applause and a standing ovation greeted this oratory.

Angerboda waved her hands for silence.

'Most of you will know that, despite appearances (*laughter*), I am now sixty-five. I have been Queen of the Witches for many years and I feel the time has come for me to step down. This year my name will not be among the nominees put forward for election. However, I have full faith in the Goddess and I know that you will elect a new Queen who is both worthy of your judgement and possessed of the physical and mental strengths required to do this job.

'As it is written in *The Very Moste Secrete Booke of Witchery*, any initiated hierophant or High Priestess who is a member of the Coven of Covens is eligible to nominate a candidate. This, as you know, is simply a step in the electoral process facilitating the promotion of interested parties. The nominator is not obliged to vote for his or her nominee, although experience has told us' – she smiled enigmatically down the table – 'that they often do . . .'

There was a risk that every single member of the Coven of Covens would nominate a candidate and vote for that candidate, thus creating a political deadlock. In fact the constitution outlined in the *Booke* circumnavigated this by forbidding the Queen to make a nomination. She remained objective, and in the event that there were even numbers she cast the deciding vote. In the (unlikely) event that deadlock should occur, the Queen was automatically exempted from re-election, for she was not allowed to vote for herself.

She continued: 'The names of the candidates will be put into the box that Merlin is bringing around and they will be announced at the end of this meeting.'

The Daughter of Branwen then stood up to give the financial report. This detailed annual outgoings (including donations to the Pagan Benevolent Fund and associated charities) and ended with information about the Sacred Bank Account which was regularly augmented by contributions, business interests, dividends from gilt-edged securities and monies bequeathed in testaments.

The Coven of Covens, the Daughter of Branwen declared proudly, was rich to the tune of six million pounds.

Jubilant clapping and stamping greeted this welcome fiscal news.

Then the wooden box in which the nominations had been placed appeared in front of Angerboda.

That time had come.

The Queen of the Witches took the hefty iron key that hung around her neck and, with a solemnity that oscillated between ceremonial decorum and an apparent fear that *The Very Moste Secrete Booke of Witchery* would explode in her face, she unlocked the padlock and opened the book.

Merlin half expected to see swarms of demons fly out and flap around the room.

Angerboda turned over the crusty pages until she found a blank folio where she could write the candidates' names, thus adding them to the hundreds of Akashic truths contained therein.

'I will announce them in the order that I open them,' she declared. 'And, as is my privilege as Queen, I will say a few words about each.'

Angerboda always delivered a polite preamble about each of the candidates. She felt it was in the interests of sportsmanship, added dignity to the competition and was helpful to those contenders who were less well known. Tradition had made these introductions somewhat perfunctory, but this year the twelve Elders seated around the table knew that the words of their sovereign would be imbued with unprecedented political importance.

'One.'

No one moved.

The branch of a tree cracked softly against a leaded window.

'Marilyn, Clan Mother of the Muses of Minehead, has been nominated by Carlisle.'

There was polite clapping and nodding of heads towards Themis, of the Handmaidens of Hermés, who bowed in acknowledgement.

'Marilyn is thirty-six years old, a Cancerian, and makes her own line of organic peanut butters.'

The members wrote this information on their pads and attempted to work out how these characteristics qualified Marilyn for the position of potentate.

'Two . . . Dame Hebadonia of the Wild Hunt has been nominated by Dublin.'

This was unexpected. Merlin was worried. He and Sheenah had been relying on the Dublin vote. Now it was likely that the Sisters of Morrighan would back their own nominee. It was a drawback, only offset by the fact that Carlisle had also made a nomination. If they had not they would certainly have followed Angerboda's lead, and Angerboda, as Merlin knew, was likely to back Myra.

'Dame Hebadonia is an Alexandrian witch from County Antrim,' said Angerboda. 'She adheres to the Celtic mystery tradition and is a regular contributor to *Witch* magazine.'

Ripple of applause.

'Three.'

Merlin held his breath.

'Sheenah, High Priestess of the Divine Order of Isis and Director of the Witches' Liberation League, has been nominated by West London.'

Loud cheers and clapping were interspersed by shouts of 'Hear Hear' and 'Jolly Good Show'.

The Norn wolf-whistled.

'Many of you will know Sheenah. She is a hereditary witch. Indeed, her grandmother served on the Coven of Covens for many years, I remember her well . . .'

The committee steeled itself for a long dissertation about Angerboda's life as a young witch and there was an imperceptible sigh of relief when she proceeded with the business in hand.

'The Witches' Liberation League,' she said, 'has been responsible for the raising of public consciousness with regard to the image of witches all over the world, and Sheenah's famous Witchcraft evening classes, the first of their kind, have trained many Wiccans who have gone on to distinguish themselves not only in their professions, but in the distances they have travelled down the path of Enlightenment.'

She wrote Sheenah's name down in the *Booke*.

'Four.'

There was no mystery as to the identity of this candidate.

'Myra, Clan Mistress of the Sisters of Diana, has been nominated by South London.'

The applause that greeted Myra's name seemed, to Merlin, to be of equal intensity to that enjoyed by Sheenah, though he noticed that Levanah did not join in the show of approval.

'Myra needs no introduction,' Angerboda said warmly. 'She is quite simply the most famous witch in the United Kingdom. As Mystic Superiority of the Sisters of Diana she has spearheaded countless conservation projects and, in her capacity as television star, she has dedicated herself tirelessly to an exhausting timetable of charity work. She is also a successful businesswoman.

'It pleases me to observe that, despite having many commitments, she still wishes to be of service. I know that she feels heartfelt allegiance to and affection for the Craft.'

Freya and Frigga, who were sitting on chairs behind their grandmother's throne and could not be seen by the assembly, made gagging faces at each other.

There was no doubt, in the eyes of the Coven of Covens, which candidate would be favoured with the influential vote of the incumbent sovereign.

Angerboda was presented with a bunch of flowers and a retirement gift of an antique athame, whose intricate carvings showed the curled body of Jörmungard, the giant serpent of Scandinavian legend.

Clapping and tears preceded the relocking of *The Very Moste Secrete Booke of Witchery*. Angerboda tapped it four times with her wand, to represent each nominee, and said:

'And now we will celebrate the Sabbat of Midsummer in our traditional way.'

Everybody obediently stood up to refresh themselves with glasses of red wine and slices of quiche.

Merlin took advantage of this section of the proceedings to gather information about the status of his candidate. Discretion was unnecessary. The election was all anyone wanted to talk about, and communicative bonhomie was unleashed by the alcohol. Eschewing the offerings of Bacchus, the Magus kept his wits about him and by the end of the party was equipped with the pertinent facts. Carlisle and Dublin intended to vote for their nominees. Marilyn and Dame Hebadonia had little hope of winning, but Merlin did not dismiss either for he knew, as outsiders, they possessed a power of their own. They were the potential recipients of strategic votes, and as alternatives to the two main parties they were attractive to those who wanted to vote for neither Sheenah nor Myra.

Bridget informed him that she intended to vote for Myra no matter how the rest of the Oracle of Queen Maeve felt about the matter (a supremist stance that was, in Merlin's view, out of character). He managed to win definite pledges for Sheenah from the Norns, the House of Phoebe and Thor's Hammer. Charles, who was rather flushed and whose crown of the Oak King had slipped rakishly to one side of his head, slapped Merlin so hard on the back that he was nearly sick.

This left Belladonna and Levanah.

Belladonna, in Merlin's opinion, was one sandwich short of the full picnic. She had a frosting of frizzled white hair, a piping little girl's voice and light blue eyes that swivelled around like lemons in a one-arm bandit. She had probably been pretty when she was ten. Merlin could see that she was the kind of woman who, when not dressed in ceremonial robes, opted for puff sleeves and pie-crust frills. He approached her knowing that avuncular interest would be more effective than joshing familiarity.

She didn't have a television, she told him proudly, so she didn't know who this Myra was. He spent a long twenty-five minutes extolling the advantages of voting for Sheenah during which Belladonna's head vibrated like a punch-ball that had just been thumped. He couldn't be sure if she had comprehended anything at all, and this opinion was corroborated later when he noticed that the twitching and swivelling continued unabated when she was standing on her own.

'What's with Belladonna?' he asked Charles.

'Dropped on her wee Sassenach heed at birth I'd weeger,' came the loud opinion.

Merlin went off to find Levanah. At least she was capable of intelligent interaction. He had always liked the leader of the Dark Women of Knowledge. A handsome woman with long, straight, dark hair and a determined jaw line, she was kind and had common sense. He was surprised, therefore, to observe that she had passed out in a chair.

He shook her awake. 'Come on, darling,' he said. 'Time for bed.'

'With you?' she slurred.

He laughed despite himself. 'I think not, dear heart. But I'll help you.'

He eased her on to her feet as if erecting the centre pole of a marquee, and prayed to his goddess Viviane that he would not have to carry the tall Dark Woman of Knowledge anywhere.

Gripping her firmly around the waist, he guided her out of the door and towards the pub where they were both staying. It was late. Stars were out and there was a crescent moon. Levanah rambled. Shop windows were reproached, lampposts were reviled and walls were held responsible as she berated Chipping Cadbury high street with a semi-coherent soliloquy. Levanah didn't know what to do . . . she could lose her job . . . Myra was a Dame Ragnell, a sarcoma . . . if she became Queen of the Witches the Astral Plane would dissolve into a quagmire of hell . . .

'So you're going to vote for Sheenah?' asked Merlin, opening the door that led to the bed and breakfast section of the Frog and Peach.

At this, Levanah burst into noisy tears and crawled on all fours up the narrow stairs in search of her bedroom.

The next morning Merlin raced to Shepherd's Bush in order to report the precise details of the Annual General Meeting, the political intrigues and the results of his informal poll.

Merlin was an efficient campaign manager but, over in Clapham, Myra's information network made the former President Nixon camp look as if it had run itself on jungle drums.

Having officially launched the CEM (Campaign for the Election of Myra) with a champagne party at the Dorchester, she had installed an 'executive' office in one of her huge guest suites on the top floor of her house. This was provided with sophisticated communications equipment including a computer, eight telephone lines and a fax machine.

Her 'heavy operations unit', recruited from the Sisters of Diana and the Daughters of Calatin, gathered information not only about each Elder of the Coven of Covens, but also each person who belonged to their home covens – the rank and file whose opinions would be instrumental in deciding the way the Elder voted. This involved surveying 240 people scattered all over the United Kingdom and Ireland. Their names, addresses and telephone numbers were filed on the computer, along with details about the backgrounds (social

123

a.   ʾpiritual), policy preferences, sexual preferences, occupations and personal ambitions. Stooges were found, sources were bought, secrets were traded. The computer was updated every day by campaign officers, each of whom was responsible for one coven. Soon there was very little that Myra's team did not know about each individual under surveillance – their financial affairs, their love affairs, how their children were doing at school. If a subject went out anywhere the supervising officer knew not only the make of car that was being driven, but the name of the final destination, whether it was Tetbury or Tahiti.

Every morning there was a staff meeting which campaign officers, liaison personnel, coordinators and senior aides attended. The campaign officers delivered reports on how much progress was being made with regard to winning the majority vote, how the balance lay within the covens themselves, and how to 'persuade' known enemies to vote for Myra. Operations officers who were out in the field and unable to attend these morning assemblies faxed their reports by 10 am.

'Knowledge is power,' Myra would say, wafting among the frenzied hurly-burly. 'Knowledge is power.'

Like Merlin, Eumonia of the Daughters of Calatin had noted the opinions held by those present at the Annual General Meeting. She relayed them to Myra from the car phone in her BMW. Assuming, she said, that Angerboda voted the way she was expected to (and was not dissuaded by her granddaughters) Myra and Sheenah had an equal chance of winning the election. The only vote that could now be described as truly floating was the one belonging to the Folkstone Faeries, a nondescript coven about which relatively little was known except for the fact that the leader seemed to be deranged and was not the owner of a television set.

Myra's wrath was terrible. She slammed down the receiver and stood in the hallway quivering. Then she picked up a Dresden shepherdess and hurled it at an eighteenth-century pier-gilt mirror. The glass shattered and a hundred tiny images of Myra's face, pale as a death mask, scattered on the floor.

She had focussed all her vital energies on becoming Queen, and the news that her immaculately coordinated campaign effort had not been fully effective slashed at the core of her being. She did not know how the Faeries had managed to slip through the net, but the person to blame would be fired the following morning. Furthermore, she would assign the entire campaign staff to the task of ensuring the support of every single member of this Folkstone cabal.

She herself, meanwhile, would take charge of the one thing that could gurantee victory.

There had been enough delay. It was time to perform the Vile Spell of Ultimate Destruction with the blood of the opponent's familiar. Only this would remove Sheenah. Permanently.

Calm now, Myra pulled out the handkerchief that she always kept down the front of her black lace bra. Flicking away the splinters of glass that had landed on the telephone, she lifted the receiver and summoned her son.

CHAPTER NINETEEN

On the day that Catty was due to be kidnapped, Steve awoke with a headache that he knew was his body's way of expressing disapproval at his collusion in the machinations of his mother. Headaches had affected him throughout his life and they were becoming worse.

As a child he had acquired the habit of complying with her demands both because he was scared of her and because he didn't know what else to do. She was bigger than him, she had a louder voice and she was possessed of a supernormal aptitude for the inspiration of guilt.

He had suffered from his first headache at the age of seven. Myra had lost her temper with the neighbour's children because they pulled faces and screamed at her every time she walked up the path to her front door. Steve, who used to stand at his bedroom window and watch them undressing Action Man and eating Marmite sandwiches, thought they looked fun. But his mother, inflamed by the damage inflicted upon her dignity, decided to cast a wart spell. Phobic abhorrence of confrontation led to a conciliatory stance, and he had obeyed her order to run after the offenders with a dead fly whose body had been impaled with a pin.

It was a spell known for its efficacy in the bringing of warts, and warts the neighbour's offspring received. Warts grew on their hands and on their faces; warts grew on their knees and elbows. Disfigured and lumpen, they looked like creatures who live on the ocean bottom and don't need the light to survive. There was no screaming and eating Marmite sandwiches after this. When the afflicted children were not being ferried to and from a series of dermatologists, they were confined to the house. Every time their mother saw Myra or

126

Steve (or Cuchulainn as he was then known), she would back away from them making the sign of the cross.

'Honestly,' Myra had said, glowing with pleasure, 'the woman shouldn't believe what she sees at the cinema.'

So Steve had been lonely. Friends were not encouraged to come home and play, and even if they had been he would have been terrified of a repeat of the wart episode.

He spent many long hours in the Temple of Diana. Standing at the altar, amidst clouds of sandalwood and mogra, Myra would develop her rituals and practise divination. To Steve, the sight of ceremonial robes made out of black silk, the veneration of a Goddess and the wearing of pentacles were normal. And quite boring.

He had been surprised when he learned that the rest of the world did not have altars in their basements, nor did they attempt to practise magic – or if they did it was more likely to be with a woollen ball underneath an eggcup rather than for the invocation of Baal and Loki. Other people's basements were full of electric drills and homemade beer, for other people, of course, had fathers.

Steve had become irredeemably confused about his own parentage when he saw men standing around at school sports days and leaving in cars with other children. It dawned on him that there were older versions of himself, and these older versions were somehow connected. How they were connected he did not know, or why.

One evening Myra had been in a good mood after one of the newspapers in which her astrology column appeared had sent her two cheques by mistake. So Steve took the opportunity to ask about his father.

The approachable temper vaporised into defensiveness followed by martyrdom. Sitting down heavily next to him, she had taken his hand dramatically into her own scented and beringed palm. After sighing for some minutes and looking out of the window, she explained that normal people had fathers, but he was not a normal person. He was the son of a witch, and he, Cuchulainn, had been the result of a magical birth, like that of his eponym.

For some time Steve had laboured under the impression that he was the offspring of a Gaelic sun god.

He read the tales of Cuchulainn's childhood and discovered that the strongest boy in the Emain Macha had once overcome a huge hound by throwing a ball into its mouth and dashing its brains out against a rock. And he learned how Cuchulainn, having left his friends Laegaire the Winner and Conall the Victorious, had courageously crossed the Plains of Ill-Luck to find the island of Scathach.

Steve had availed himself of the personality of the Hound of Ulster. Not only did he grow his hair long, like that of his Irish hero, but he took to playing hurley, or hockey, as he had seen the pictures divulge. However, when a schoolteacher had come across him waving a school dinner knife at a bird sitting on a telegraph wire and received the explanation that it was the Morrighan come to help him in battle, the man had written to Myra and suggested that the child see a psychiatrist, for surely at the age of fifteen he was too old to be playing such games.

So Myra had admitted to her son that he was not, in fact, the protagonist of the court of King Conchobar, but the son of a person called Harold, who had deserted them and was an evil daemon without conscience or morality and who, as far as she knew, was dead.

This revelation had an even more stimulating effect on Steve's imagination than the tale of Celtic myth. He became obsessed with the monster called Harold and could think of little else. Then, during one summer holiday, his mother had left him alone for the day while she went to inspect some Sèvres china in a Bournemouth antique shop. Rifling through her desk for evidence of the daemon's identity, he had found a wad of letters and photographs bound together with an elastic band.

Nervous, but patient, he had inspected the pictures one by one. There were many of himself as a baby, looking discoloured and feminine, and there were portraits of various members of the Order of Diana standing next to burned trees that were believed to be the arboreal effigies of obscure Saxon nature deities. There was one of his mother, at the age of eighteen, in a chorus line of women wearing jewelled bathing costumes, and some of her standing next to a white-haired man he knew to be Gerald Gardner. Then he had come to an image that made the blood bang around his body. His mother, very beautiful, with dark hair and thick eyeliner that emphasised the oriental slant of her features, stood next to a bald man who, slightly shorter than her, gazed out of the picture with the black eyes that Steve knew to be his own.

Transfixed for some minutes by this paper memory, he had flicked over the photograph to see his mother's handwritten explanation: 'Me and Harold. Beltane 1961.'

Relieved in a way that his father was bald rather than de-monic, Steve had resisted the urge to steal the photograph and hide it.

Now here he was again, still confused, still doing his mother's bidding despite the voice of his inner self, still fearful of the terrible shouting.

Sighing, he packed a rucksack with the tools he thought he would need – rope, Sellotape, sedatives and a wicker basket that he hoped would be big (and strong) enough to sustain the spitting nightmare.

He knew that today, Saturday, Sheenah would attend a committee meeting of the Witches' Liberation League and that Catty, due to the instability of her nature, would remain locked in the house.

At 5.30 he drove his van into Sheenah's street and parked it far enough from her house to remain unobserved but near enough to see her front door. At 6 pm she locked the house and he saw her sweep off down the road, cloak, robes and hair flowing behind her in the summer breeze.

Steve unlatched the side door leading into the garden and walked around to the window that opened into the kitchen. He reached up and easily removed the ancient plastic disc of the extracter fan then, pushing his arm through the clean circular hole, he opened the catch to the window and climbed in on top of the sink.

Easy.

Not so easy, however, was the location of Sheenah's famil-iar. She was not squashed into her basket in the kitchen, nor was her giant nose pressed into the mountain of chopped liver that had been left in her dinner bowl.

'Catty,' whispered Steve. 'Catty, where are you?'

He padded into the temple which was next to the kitchen. Nothing.

He crept upstairs to Sheenah's office. Nothing.

With a heavy heart, he climbed further into the crepuscular gloom that was the top portion of Sheenah's house and where he assumed her bedroom would be.

'Catty,' Steve sang softly.

He peered into a bathroom where there was a doll with a flouncy lace dress pretending she wasn't a loo roll. Then he walked into what was obviously the master bedroom.

In one corner, where a fire might have been, there was a shrine and against another wall was a chest of drawers on which there were rows of framed photographs. There were pictures of witches and children, and of Sheenah's grandmother standing in the middle of her vegetable garden. Then he saw one which made his heart stop. There, standing with his arms around Sheenah, was a photograph of his father.

What was Harold doing on top of Sheenah's chest of drawers? And why were he and Sheenah involved in a passionate embrace?

Reminding himself that he was in the middle of committing an illegal act and that it would be best to accomplish it as soon as possible, he wrenched his eyes away from the picture of Harold and repressed the questions that battered his mind.

Catty, despite being well on her way to becoming addicted to barbiturates and consequently a victim of the paranoia that this entails, was still capable of rational thought. Her large brain told her not to trust anybody who crept surreptitiously around the house.

Aware suddenly that he was not alone in the room, Steve swung around to see the cat sitting upright in the middle of Sheenah's bed. Her yellow eyes flashed like citrines.

'Catty?' he whispered encouragingly.

Catty spat.

'Catty, come here.'

Catty's claws ripped into the pink sateen coverlet and her hackles rose.

Oh, Christ, thought Steve.

'Catty,' he persevered, staring straight into the gleaming citrines. 'Catty, Catty, Catty. Lovely Catty, you are a beauty...'

He continued staring at her, unblinking, crooning her name until she started to rock from side to side in rhythm with the sound of his exhortation.

'Go to sleep, Catty, go to sleep.'

It was too much. The feline fiend slumped into an unconscious heap on the bed and Steve, staggering under the weight of her body, managed to pour her into the wicker basket.

He half ran, half crept down the stairs, wiped his footprints off the sink, wiped the windows and climbed out. Then he replaced the catch and the air vent.

Checking that there were no observant neighbourhood watch schemes, Steve sidled out through the garden door.

Catty did not so much as twitch throughout the journey from Shepherd's Bush to Clapham.

CHAPTER TWENTY

When Sheenah returned from the committee meeting of the Witches' Liberation League and couldn't see Catty, her first reaction was one of relief. Mellowed by the effects of many glasses of Yvette's apple and elderberry champagne, she went to bed under the impression that Catty was either sulking or hiding.

The next morning, when breakfast failed to herald the rematerialisation of her familiar, Sheenah began a search. There was no sign of her anywhere. Thinking that Catty might have escaped, she checked every window in the house, including the skylight in the loft, to find that they were firmly locked. She did not see how Catty, a phenomenon though she was, could possibly have broken out.

The implications of the situation began to dawn on Sheenah. First of all, Catty was dangerous and she wore Sheenah's name and address on a gold disc around her neck. The witch's forehead furrowed as she considered the series of recriminatory court cases in which she might become involved.

Secondly, the circumstances were very suspicious: the house must have been broken into, but there were no physical traces of forced entrance.

She rang Cuthbert. Although he was no longer a member of the force, she hoped that his police training had included techniques of detection that would enable him to proffer some educated suggestions.

Cuthbert stomped around the house checking all the windows and writing notes in a small black book as he had been taught at Hendon. Then he descended to the kitchen.

'You have an air vent, I see.'

'Yes,' said Sheenah.

'Well, if there was a thief, and I think there was, he would have removed the air vent and put his arm through the window. It happens in Shepherd's Bush all the time. Most break-ins round here are done like that.'

'But why should anyone burgle Catty and not the television or the radio or my jewellery?'

Cuthbert was mystified.

Sheenah rang Merlin.

'Oh my Gods!' he said when she told him.

'What? What?'

'It was probably Myra.'

'Myra? What on earth would she want with Catty?'

The truth dawned on her as the words left her mouth. They both spoke together.

'Black magic.'

Sheenah felt faint.

'What am I going to do? Catty will be in the most terrible danger if Myra is practising black magic.'

'If Myra is practising black magic, she will be disqualified immediately from the Queen of the Witches,' observed Merlin.

'I know. But how can we expose her? I have no proof. No one will believe me. They'll think it's propaganda, that I'm just trying to win the election by conducting a smear campaign.'

'I'll be around in a tick,' said Merlin. 'Don't worry. We can handle this. Remember what Catty is like. The pill will be wearing off, she'll be strong *and* violent. The Princes of Darkness would be wise to leave well alone.'

Sheenah sat down at her kitchen table and rested her head in her hands. She had been flattered when the witches of West London had endorsed her nomination, and pleased by the support she had received from the electorate. Until now, she had seen the contest merely as a challenge which might or might not end in a job that would open new horizons. If she had envisaged a power struggle such as this, Sheenah would never have allowed Merlin to persuade her to run for office. And now, because she had been blind to the reality of the situation, her familiar was in danger of being murdered.

133

Terrible though Catty was, they had known each other for a long time and had shared a life. As she thought of Catty helplessly suffering the atrocities meted out by Myra's cold psychosis, fear and grief slowly matured into resentment, and resentment turned to rage.

Sheenah might have stepped down from the election had it not been for this incident. Now she was obliged to stand up to Myra, if only because she was the only person in a position to prevent the black witch from ascending to a rank that would allow her to develop her malevolence into a force against which there could be no opponent.

The Magus arrived with a pile of books dedicated to the revelation of thaumaturgical knowledge, a brown paper bag full of garlic, a cross whose prongs were of equal length and a cardboard canister full of sea salt.

Together they studied the myriad tales of etheric offensiveness that are rife in the history of occultism.

Merlin sat behind a red and gold edition of Frater Marduk's classic *Magickal Martial Arts*. The book was so big that the only evidence of the reader's presence were the smoke rings puffed from his menthylated More cigarette.

'Have you experienced an unnatural lack of energy?' he asked.

'No,' said Sheenah, who was making notes from *Astral Protection – Seven Steps to Celestial Security*.

'Any odd or evil smells about the place?'

'No more than usual.'

'Strange knockings or tappings?'

'No.'

'Nightmares?'

'A few.'

'Run of bad luck?'

Sheenah took a sip of lager.

'Well. Poor Melinda dying, and the robin. Then there was the fuss with Cuthbert and Rosaleen. That's never happened to me before . . . Yes.' She nodded. 'I have had a run of bad luck.'

'You know we're going to have to confront that nark, Steve,' said Merlin, lowering Frater Marduk and snorting More

134

smoke angrily through his nostrils. 'I bet he's responsible for a lot of this. Why else would Myra plant him here?'

'You're right,' she agreed. 'But I still cannot believe that Harold's son is evil.'

'Huh!' Merlin curled his lip so that his white moustache danced the Dying Swan. 'I'm not so sure. He's got Harold's eyes. And remember what Harold's eyes could do. Imagine! The mixture of Harold's powers of mesmerism and the magickal knowledge of Myra. The frightfulness makes one shudder.'

'I wonder if he knows I was once married to his father,' said Sheenah mistily, for she was thinking of how in love they had been, Harold and she, that first summer when they had gone to Stonehenge in the Dormobile. He had played 'Green Grow the Rushes-O' on the recorder and mended the camp stove when it had disintegrated. He had been very good with his hands, she remembered fondly.

Sheenah and Merlin ate lunch, and spent the afternoon performing rituals of protection against the battery of astral missiles Sheenah expected to receive. Psychic warfare could be dangerous, if not lethal, and she knew that these precautionary methods were vital if it was true that Myra had kidnapped Catty.

'We'll have to draw on the Christ Force,' apologised Merlin, peering into Frater Marduk's volume of advice. 'It's not aligned with the Wiccan path, I'm afraid, but in the end it's the one that all the adepts advise. It's trustworthy, you see. It's the only one you can be sure will be on the side of Good.'

So they went to Sheenah's temple and, standing upright, they faced east. Sheenah steadied her own vibrations and purified her aura of thoughts of revenge. Then she made the Cabalistic cross on her breast and brow and said, 'To Thee, oh God, be the Kingdom and the Power and the Glory unto the Ages of Ages. Amen.'

Imagining that she was holding a mighty sword, she continued, 'In the name of God I take in hand the Sword of Power for defence against evil and aggression.' She saw herself grow to twice her natural height so that she became ten foot ten, a tremendous armed and unassailable figure vibrating with the powers of the Almighty.

They both walked in a Magic Circle around the altar, imagining a line of flames as they did so; then, stepping over it, they stood side by side, palms together.

'May the mighty Archangel Raphael protect me from all evil approaching from the east,' she prayed and repeated the request with regard to the mighty Archangels Gabriel (west), Michael (south) and Uriel (north).

While Merlin placed cloves of garlic and saucers of nitric acid all over the house, Sheenah went off to have a protective and cleansing bath.

She tipped the canister of sea salt into the water and consecrated it with the words:

'I exorcise thee, Creature of Earth, by the Living God, by the Holy God, by the omnipotent God, that thou mayest be purified of all evil influences in the name of Adonai, who is Lord of Angels and of men.'

Then she marked a cross on her forehead, undressed and said:

'In the name which above every other name and in the power of the Father and of the Son and of the Holy Ghost I exorcise all influences and seeds of evil.'

After full immersion in these magical waves she put on a clean maroon jellabah and, with the help of Merlin, moved the direction of her bed, as this was also known to confuse unpleasant visitants.

'Well,' gasped her friend, who was by now exhausted, 'I think we've done everything we can.'

They spent the rest of the day plotting how to retrieve Catty.

CHAPTER TWENTY-ONE

A person as skilled in the art of necromancy as Myra knew that much preparation is required for a ritual to terminate opposition. Thus, for a week before the date of Catty's abduction, she had spent the evenings in the inner sanctum of her Black Temple preparing the Satanic Majesties for the arrival of their sacrifice, and performing subsidiary spells that she knew would flatter them and encourage their support.

Lighting a fire underneath her cauldron, she set it beneath a statue of Vulcan, the Jeweller of the Gods who puts force into sorcery. As the water bubbled to the boil she threw in white mullein, galangal root, angelica and Solomon's seal. Breathing their acrid essences deep into her lungs, she cried out the infernal names of Enochian diablerie – Astratoth who rides a dragon, Bune who has three heads (human, griffin and dog) and Murmur. Exhorting them to 'banish all foul enemies', she snatched one of the rusting nails which she had stolen from a graveyard in Slough. Holding the feathered body of a dead Mandarin duck above the burning cauldron, she stabbed the bird repeatedly in the chest.

Myra knew that rites such as these would awaken the Wise Ones of the Bottomless Pit and motivate them to do her bidding, but she also knew that the Princes of the Night (and Choronzon in particular) were fickle creatures. They had been known, when dissatisfied, to work their ghastliness on the very person who had invoked them. So, on the sixth night, she drank red wine, ate a communion wafer and, kneeling down in front of the altar, said:

'I take the Benediction of Pandaemonium, O Lords of the Inferno, that they may preserve me from fumes of sordidity or spirits of evil should they be cast up in the course of my careful conjuration.'

By the end of a week of incantations, infernal rites, burning soups of Vulcan and yelling at the Mysterious Lords, the Black Temple of Myra exuded a Lethean atmosphere. Shadows of disembodied animals flickered across the walls, there was a smell of drains and the temperature was hyperborean. At midnight, on the sixth night, a crack appeared down the northern wall, the domain of Leviathan, and Myra knew They were waiting for the Grand Gesture.

She polished the silver chalice from which she would drink the blood of Sheenah's Catty, and consecrated the dagger which she had bought from a member of the Church of Satan in California who was a forensic scientist and had stolen it after a case involving a serial killer on Venice Beach.

Myra was ready.

Sheenah's time had come.

The paladins of the Left-hand Path would vanquish the weak and pathetic supplicants of the Right-hand Path.

And she would be Queen.

Myra was concealed in the Black Temple when Steve returned from his felonious expedition. He told Athene, who had answered the door, to watch the hamper, for he could not predict when the hypnotic trance would lift and Catty would regain consciousness. 'I'll come back later,' he said, for he hoped both to replace the cat, unobserved, in Sheenah's house, and to accost his mother about the matter of his father's photograph on Sheenah's chest of drawers.

Noting the opportune presence of a waning moon suitable for spells designed to cause distress, Myra grabbed the wicker container and placed it in the middle of the inverted pentagram that had been painted around the altar. Then she lit two black candles and made the sign of the Sun.

'In nomine dei nostri Satanas Luciferi excelsi,' she muttered as she disrobed.

Fortifying herself with gulps from a pewter tankard full of wine, she took a small drum and slapped it with the palm of her hand, slowly at first, then faster and faster, and, as the staccato tattoo cracked around the gloomy temple, her body spiralled and twisted in a frenzied dance. Drumming, stamping, she bobbed up and down until at last she fell, chest heaving, blood pumping, on her knees in front of the basket. Entranced by the powers of her own invocation and palpitating with hatred, envy and bile, she shrieked out the Vile Spell of Ultimate Destruction:

'Behold! O Lords of Mortal Horror and dwellers of brackish pits! Hear my chorus of vengeance and see my bloody sacrifice. I call for Choronzon, Messenger of Death, Master of Disorder, to slither forth and lacerate this enemy of mine. I call for scorpions to sting, fires to burn and knives to scar until the Witch of Isis falls down and weeps with torment. Come forth, ye sour fiends and vile demons, ye wraiths of Dis who care only for vice and pain. Come forth with thine bifid barbs and rid me of this dismal foe.'

Catty, like all neurotics, was a light sleeper, and this characteristic did not alter under the spell of hypnosis. She awoke to see a naked harridan leaning over her screaming about scorpions and threatening her with a knife.

It was not a scene guaranteed to smooth her already considerably ruffled fur.

She sprang out of the basket and flung herself against her tormentor.

Myra, unbalanced by the weight of the sacrificial victim's body, which landed on her shoulder, fell heavily to the temple floor where a sudden fierce stabbing pierced through her right shoulder.

The dagger clattered beside her.

Flexing the claws that had held so many in terror, Catty slashed Myra down her back leaving four streaks of oozing blood.

Yelling with fear, Myra called out to Choronzon and the Infernal Hierarchy to help her fight the venom and fury of this Creature from Hell, but the Archfiends and profligate satyrs either realised that this was a being against which they could hold no sway, or they were busy elsewhere causing car crashes and making it rain on people's wedding days. No helpful wraith was sent by the Masters to protect the Mistress of the Stars.

Blowing her body out to twice its already abnormal size, Catty spat and rasped at the cowering and bloody Myra. Then, with a sound like that of a ward of crying babies, she leaped out of the magical pentagram, disappeared through the door, up the stairs and out of the window. Pelting down the pavement in a blur of fur, she hurled herself against Steve's lower calves, bowling him over on the pavement outside Myra's house.

Although he did not actually see what had knocked him down, an educated guess was supported by the sight of a small droplet of blood on the white marble steps that led up to the front door.

Nervously, Steve let himself in.

The house was dark. The servants had gone to bed.

'Mother!' he shouted.

Silence.

'Where are you?'

Silence.

He saw, to his alarm, that another viscid spot of blood glistened on the cream pile of the carpet.

Heart racing, he dashed down the stairs to the Temple.

But there was nobody in the Temple of Diana. He surveyed the discarded and dusty athames, the bowls of dead flowers, the unkempt statues of Diana and Demeter, the empty candle holders, and he felt the first stirrings of suspicion. No ceremonial sabbats or seasonal rites had been practised in this temple for many months. Furthermore, there was a disgusting smell of sewers emanating from a curtain behind the altar. He pulled the red velvet aside to see a damp corridor and hear the sound of moaning.

He inched his body through.

And here, in her Black Temple of Evil, lay Myra, bloody, unconscious and naked on the floor.

Steve shuddered as he entered this terrible place. He saw the shadows of demons, smelt the cloacal vapours and felt the oppression of menace.

'Mother!' he shouted.

He ran over to her, crossing himself as he stepped over the lines and into the gruesome domain defined by the pentagram. As he knelt over her, a thousand cold fingers dug into his chest and neck.

Myra groaned.

140

He picked her up, carried her out of the profane chapel, through the Temple of Diana and up to her bedroom where he laid her down and thanked God she wasn't dead.

She came round as he was painting an antiseptic lotion on to the wounds streaked down her back.

'Aaaagh,' she wailed. 'What happened?'

'The cat escaped,' he said furiously, 'and you passed out.'

'Bloody hell! I think I've dislocated my shoulder. You're going to have to call the doctor,' she said, face white with pain.

'I can't believe what I've seen,' he said coldly. 'How long have you been involved in black magic?'

'Oh, don't be so naive, darling,' she said, falling back on to her lace pillow. 'There's very little difference between black and white magic. The Forces are neutral. If you call on them they'll help, that's all there is to it.'

'Bollocks! That's the typical sophist statement of a Satanist, and you know it. And if it's so innocent, how come you've been hiding it?'

'The world does not understand witches, or magic, or anything it cannot see,' she said. 'I happen to be good at black magic, I like its symbolism and I've been practising it since your father left. It was certainly responsible for making enough money for your education.'

'Yeah? Well, I would have been just as happy at Holland Park Comprehensive,' said Steve. 'I can't believe you could be so stupid. Black magicians always die in terrible circumstances, you know that.'

'Oh, do shut up.'

'I can't believe it.' He shook his head and got up from the bed where he had been sitting. He walked over to the window and looked out, watching his breath form an opaque circle on the pane. 'And what,' he said quietly, 'was a picture of my father doing on Sheenah's chest of drawers?'

Myra started. She had not appreciated that Cuchulainn knew what his father looked like. She was capable of long and convincing argument in support of the black arts, but she was aware that the events surrounding her marriage to Harold would be less easy to cast in a flattering light.

'Sheenah knew Harold. We lived near each other in Battersea Rise.'

141

'So what were their arms doing around each other?'

'They were friends.'

'Don't lie to me, Mother. I'm sick of it.'

Myra lost her temper. Her screech was a weapon designed to instil tremors to the nether regions of any opponent's heart. Adrenalin pumped around Steve's body preparing it for fight or flight.

In the past he had fled.

'SHEENAH AND HAROLD KNEW EACH OTHER. SO THE FUCK WHAT? THE ONLY THING THAT IS YOUR BUSINESS IS THE FACT THAT THE BASTARD LEFT. NOW GET OUT AND GET ME A FUCKING DOCTOR!'

Steve glared at his mother and his anger fermented. This time, however, he did not intend to leave the room with the feeling that something inside him was decaying.

He drew his hand back and slapped her sharply across the face.

She fell silent.

His black eyes glinted.

'If you won't tell me,' he said icily, 'Sheenah will.'

He left the room.

Myra slumped back on her pillow. The pain in her shoulder throbbed and the mark of her son's hand grew livid against the pallor of her face.

CHAPTER TWENTY-TWO

Dig was withdrawing.

Police pressure had forced his contact to return to South America, leaving him bereft of the narcotics with which he had sustained his large clientele. The queues of junkies, amiable when there was a consistent supply at reasonable prices, had been transformed into a dangerous mob. Some of them threatened physical violence, others stole the carpets, several had moved in to wait until Dig made a new connection.

Dig's nose ran and he shook with cold, despite the fact that the heating was on high and it was July (as far as he could remember). His body had grown accustomed to the warmth provided by heroin, and his mind attuned to a perspective which was never assaulted by the unpleasant aspects of normality. Now he felt as if his muscles were closing in on themselves and, when not disorientated, he was gripped with a terrible longing.

This insalubrious scenario reached its nadir the morning that Hugh Hope (known, inevitably, as 'Hopeless') and (Lord) Phoenix Warburton arrived.

They had been drinking all night in a shebeen in Westbourne Park Road, and exuded a putrid mixture of old beer and unwashed skin.

Phoenix Warburton was an enormous peer, whose behemothian proportions were inadequately contained by an ensemble that included a tight old tweed jacket, filthy corduroy trousers and buttonless Viyella shirt through which his stomach was usually poking.

He had, after years of drug abuse, come to the conclusion that being a lord made one not only different but also better than the rest of the human race. Indefatigably impressed by his own lineage, he had not spoken to his brother for twenty years because he refused to use his title when addressing him.

When he was eighteen, he had appeared at the front desk of Christie's with a family Canaletto which he had sold to pay for his habit. The Canaletto had been followed by other important artworks, until the Warburton estate had disappeared up the endless tunnel that was the Warburton nose and into the indestructible genetic inheritance that was the Warburton constitution.

Hugh Hope had long been his penniless but enthusiastic sidekick.

The antics of Warburton and 'Hopeless' were the stuff of legend, for the duo were celebrated by those sectors of London social life that enjoyed living vicariously.

Dig's front door had been ripped off its hinges some weeks before, so entrance was easy for the drunken pair.

Warburton toppled into the flat followed by Hope, and they launched into a complicated psychodrama that began with them shouting that they loved each other and the world and always would. This was immediately followed by terrible insults about each other's sexual proclivities and the finale was a punch-up on the sofa.

Dig looked on helplessly as the few remaining lamps were smashed to pieces.

Deciding he had better join them, he swallowed a glass of Jack Daniels and stuffed the last of his valued stash into a bong.

Phoenix Warburton urinated into the kitchen sink.

They wanted drugs and they needed cash. They were desperate. And Dig, his craving awakened by the whisky, felt the same.

Finally he agreed that they should go upstairs and persuade Rosaleen to advance them some money. 'And,' leered Phoenix Warburton, 'we might give her one as well.'

Dig seemed to recall that he already had, but couldn't be sure. His faculties had been undermined by fatigue, the shock of seeing Phoenix Warburton lumbering madly around his flat and the chemical optimism precipitated by the early morning Jack Daniels.

Rosaleen's faculties, relatively intact, had been entertained by a morning in the bath and a long reverie. Andrew had flown to L.A. before she had had time to tell him that she did not wish to marry him. After much staring out of the window she had written him several letters of varying length and clarity. The final version was friendly but failed to give any specific reasons for her decision. Inclining towards diplomacy rather than honesty, she had decided not to allude to Steve who, despite his extreme wierdness, was retaining a stranglehold on her emotions.

Part of her hoped that Andrew, deranged by this blow, would continue to pursue her with pathetic fealty, but knowledge of his indestructible morale informed her that he would not take this repudiation to heart.

She was relieved it was Sunday. Perhaps there would be a short respite from the fantastic timetable of social engagements that was now controlling her life.

She was putting on a white towelling bathrobe and had scraped her wet hair into a hideous yellow turban when the door bell rang for a very long time, owing to the mammoth physique of Phoenix Warburton leaning heavily upon it.

Rosaleen recognised him from a number of charity balls she had attended, at which he had been arrested for causing an affray. Standing with him was Dig, stooped and glaucous, and a small pointed man wearing a pair of tight white jeans through which one could see the minute mouldings of his groin.

They did not wait to be invited in, but pushed past her.

'Hurrow,' said Phoenix Warburton, breathing a sirocco of alcohol into her face and pressing his barrel stomach against her.

Rosaleen gasped.

'What do you want?' she said as calmly as was possible.

'We need to borrow five hundred quid.'

'I don't have five hundred, er, quid,' she said. 'What do you want it for anyway?'

She knew Phoenix Warburton's reputation. Everybody knew Phoenix Warburton's reputation. He had received six months for GBH, for a start. She wondered what he was doing with Dig. She wondered who the indescribably nasty individual in tight trousers was, and she wondered how she was going to eject them from her house without money and without violence.

' 'Course you got five hundred quid,' rasped the dilapidated lord. The definition of his ancestral features had crumpled under the pressure of the toxins to which they had been subjected. 'Everyone's got five hundred quid.'

Rosaleen resisted the impulse to say that he obviously hadn't.

Warburton's emaciated accomplice proceeded to search the house for cash. He looked under sofas, he turned vases upside down, he peered into the microwave and washing machine, he found her Kelly bag and showered its contents on to the floor.

'She's got a fucking gold credit card!' he yelled.

Rosaleen rotated her head in order that her vision would be less impaired by Phoenix Warburton's chest and saw Hugh Hope wave the plastic in the air and then slowly ooze to the floor where he remained immobile, except for the occasional twitch.

'Dig,' said Rosaleen, 'what the hell is going on?'

Dig was shivering but felt as if he had a temperature of 104.

'It's only a loan,' he snivelled. 'We'll pay it back next week.'

' 'Course we will!' shouted Phoenix Warburton, pressing himself with greater vigour against her. 'You can trust me. I'm a peer of the realm.'

'I haven't got the cash,' Rosaleen said.

'In that case,' Warburton suggested, with the constructive cunning of the addict, 'you give us your card and ID number and we'll go and get the money from the machine in the wall.'

'That's extortion.'

'Look,' he sneered, 'you haven't much choice.'

His small, arrogant eyes flickered dangerously in flaccid cheeks. Gazing at her with contempt, he put his hand down the front of her bathrobe and rubbed her breast. Bile and fear rose in Rosaleen. She tried desperately to push him off, hands beating hopelessly against his podgy, immobile body. Then she felt his other hand, wet, cold and smelling of ancient nicotine, close tightly around her throat. Blood pumped into her head and her senses dissolved into disbelief, followed, as the constriction intensified around her windpipe, by no feeling except the struggle to breathe.

Phoenix Warburton was going to kill her.

'Leave her alone,' said Dig sadly.

'Fuck off.'

The pressure increased.

The room began to blur.

'Yes,' said another voice. 'Leave her alone.'

Phoenix Warburton swung around to see a tall stranger whose hair was stuck out at right angles to his head.

'Steve!' gasped Rosaleen as her assailant's fingers released their grip. She fell forward, rubbing her throat and retching.

Steve's appearance bore little resemblance to his normal physiognomy, for he had turned into Cu Cuchulainn, the Hound of Ulster, and was thus the beneficiary of invincible might. His chest had extended to the size of a galleon, his eyes flashed like brilliantines, his legs were as thick as oak trees and the knuckles of his mammoth fists glowed like white cogs.

There was no crimson tunic bound with a brooch whose light blinded all who looked upon it, and there was no hereditary vestment of russet silk. Steve had not received warrior training under the instructions of the lonely woman of Scathach, and he was not armed with the gae bulga or even the sword of Fergus mac Roich that stretched to the length of a rainbow. But it did seem that the Four Elements, the Seven Planets and Sun God had empowered him with the frenzied battle fury of Celtic myth. He had suffered his riastradh and was now a fearsome, multiform and hitherto unknown being.

But, as we have heard, it was the eyes of Steve the Champion that were his most powerful weapons.

'Leave her alone,' he repeated, and his black irises dug into his opponent.

'What the fuck,' spat Phoenix Warburton, 'has it got to do with you?'

There are some people in this world who are resilient to the forces of hypnotism. They refuse, as it were, to go under. There are no uniform characteristics that enable them to be identified. They are not more stupid or clever, sensitive or insensitive than anyone else, they just happen to be bad subjects. Catty was not one of these individuals. Phoenix Warburton was. Unaffected by Steve's mesmerism, he lunged forward with the intention of pushing him over and kicking his head in.

Steve stepped aside.

The full weight of Warburton's swollen body, increased by the speed at which it was travelling, crashed into the opposite wall of the hallway.

He was knocked unconscious.

Steve turned to Dig. 'You had better go.'

Dig slunk away.

Rosaleen sat down on the stairs, grabbed the yellow turban from her head, threw it furiously to the floor and wept loudly.

Steve sat down beside her and put his arms around her heaving shoulders. His figure had returned to its normal proportions and his hair was flat upon his head.

'We'd better call a doctor,' he said.

Rosaleen sobbed.

After an ambulance had removed the supine bodies of Phoenix Warburton and Hugh Hope, Steve told Rosaleen everything, for he knew now that all this must come to an end. His mother must not be allowed to continue either with her nefarious practices or in her bid to take over the Coven of Covens.

He described his part in the intelligence operation, including the theft of Catty. He divested the details of Myra's Black Temple and the cat's brush with death that had been the result of his credulity and weakness. He explained, without denunciation, some of the mitigating circumstances and ended with the mystery of his father's image in Sheenah's house.

'So she told the newspapers about Cuthbert?' asked Rosaleen.

'I suppose so, yes,' he said.

Rosaleen assimilated this long monologue of astonishing information, appreciated the courage that was required to make such a confession, and was flattered that she had been entrusted to hear it.

Although much was difficult to comprehend, she sympathised. Anybody's judgement would have been impaired by close contact with a woman whose manner was so intemperate and whose deeds were so chilling. It was a miracle that Steve was not raving.

'Sheenah must be told,' she said.

'I hope she won't prosecute.'

Rosaleen stood up, placed her face close to his and pushed her hand gently through his hair. He hugged her.

Somewhere far away, very far away, she heard a mystical sound. It was not, she thought, the music of the spheres, but the triumphant chords of a church organ which was playing 'The Bridal Chorus' from Wagner's 'Lohengrin'.

CHAPTER TWENTY-THREE

It was Sunday evening. The summer sun was crawling lazily out of the kitchen and gold spots shimmied about on saucepans and the silver knobs of the gas cooker. The smell of nitric acid and garlic mingled with that of the fresh coffee Cuthbert, Sheenah and Merlin were drinking from a large cafetière. They were airing a selection of plans, of varying feasibility, designed to retrieve Catty and expose Myra.

'Are you aware,' said Cuthbert, who was happy now he had been accepted as a trainee inspector by the RSPCA, 'that if an animal has been maltreated the police can prosecute under the 1911 Protection of Animals Act?'

'How many years will Myra get for kidnap?' said Sheenah bitterly.

'Or catricide,' added Merlin.

'I don't know,' answered Cuthbert, who had not been born with an ear for the nuances of irony.

'I suppose I could go and confront her,' said Sheenah, balking at this thought.

'She'll only deny everything,' said Merlin. 'It would be completely pointless.'

'Poor Catty. I can't bear it.'

Sheenah wondered if there were any Halcion left in the packet.

'I'd just like to know how they got her out of the house,' mused Merlin, lighting up a More and puffing on it with a philosopher's deliberation. 'Only an experienced racketeer would be brave enough to abduct that excuse for a domestic pet.'

'Perhaps it was a gang,' said Cuthbert.

'Don't be so mean,' said Sheenah. 'Catty might be dead for all we know. Myra might be drinking her blood as we speak.'

Merlin felt sick.

'So black magic does exist,' said Cuthbert. 'I thought it was something made up by the newspapers.'

'The problem with magic in general,' explained the experienced High Priestess, 'is that it tends to attract those who wish to fulfil their own ends, good or bad, and in the hands of brutes and egomaniacs the Forces of the Ether can become very dangerous indeed.'

'Mind you,' Merlin observed, 'I can't think of one black magician who is an attractive advertisement for the practice. They're never rich or lovely, or even happy.'

'Nevertheless,' said Sheenah, 'that is why we witches must be so careful. That is why those who wish to learn the Craft must be properly vetted and trained. The Secrets are powerful. Not everybody can cope with them.'

'No,' agreed Merlin. 'If everyone knew the Secrets, all hell would break loose. And I mean Hell.'

'Which is why the Coven of Covens is so against black magic,' said Sheenah, 'and quite right too. It's all very well being libertarian about people's spiritual paths but black magic panders to base instincts. Indeed, it encourages them. I believe it is the responsibility of the individual to evolve. White magic is an aid to this. It raises positive energy and its object is to heal. The Wiccan way should help people overcome their personal defects for their own as well as the common good. Those who deviate bring calumny on the rest of us. People still think that to be a witch is to worship the Devil, and it only needs one person to be exposed doing exactly that, or practising the kind of rite that I believe Myra has been practising, and the Craft could be set back hundreds of years. It confirms what the public suspects of any group with a reputation for secrecy, and the public enjoys being horrified. The Liberation League has worked hard to rectify the damage caused by years of hatred and abuse, but this could be destroyed overnight. One furious bishop will write to *The Times* and Parliament will start talking about revoking the law. Before you know it we'll be back to the Burning Times.'

151

Cuthbert's face fell into serious repose as he considered the horrors of this prospect.

Merlin looked at Sheenah, and knew he was correct in his conviction that she would be a remarkable Queen of the Witches.

'Yes,' he said, guiding his thin tail of ash carefully over a glass ashtray, 'Myra has let the side down very badly indeed.'

'Angerboda should be told as soon as possible,' Sheenah continued. 'But how in the name of Tezeatlipoca can we prove it? I'd consider attempting to bribe one of the Daughters of Calatin, but they might not know anything and anyway I don't want to sink to *her* level.'

'Quite right,' concurred Merlin.

He had opened his mouth to add a point about the necessity of retaining one's self-respect when he was interrupted by the first twelve bars of 'Seventy-Six Trombones', which was Sheenah's front door bell.

The witch leaped to answer it, certain there was going to be news about Catty. Her powers of precognition were correct in this assumption, although not quite in the form she had envisaged.

'Oh, hullo,' she said coldly. 'You'd better come in.'

'I have to talk to you,' said Steve.

'Yes,' she answered. 'I should think you do. Where's my Catty?'

She waved him into her office because this interview required a formal atmosphere.

He stood in front of her staring down at his feet and hating himself. Not wishing to be forced to endure the painful silence that tends to precede confession, and impatient to hear the truth, Sheenah spoke first.

'I assume Myra has her.'

'Well – ' Steve cleared his throat nervously and felt the knots of nervousness tighten deep within his abdomen. 'She did have. But Catty escaped.'

'Thank the Great Goddess for small blessings!'

She waited for an explanation.

'I am Myra's son.'

'I know.'

Steve stared at her. 'Why didn't you say anything?'

152

She stared back with determination setting her chin. Steve appreciated for the first time that underneath this rotund eccentric there was a powerful woman, a powerful woman who did not take the offensive unless maliciously wounded.

'The time didn't seem right,' she told him coolly.

'Harold is my father.'

'Yes.'

'Were you a friend of his?'

'He was my husband.'

Steve sat down on the swivel chair in front of the computer. The sun had set. It was dark and the windows looked as if they had been coated with black paint.

He knew so little about this man, Harold. He wondered what had happened all those years ago, what had prompted his father to leave one woman in order to marry another. The personalities of Sheenah and Myra seemed to be incomparable.

The significance of his role was now clear to him. Docility, it seemed, was dangerous. By permitting his mother to subvert the course of his natural instinct he had allowed her to mould him to a shape that was her own cast. He had become her henchman and his potential for deviance had been easily stirred. Yet despite the discomfort of these painful revelations, he wished he could remove himself from blame. He wanted Sheenah to like him. He wanted everyone to like him.

'I see,' he said. 'I'm sorry. I didn't know. I really didn't. I never met him, you know.'

'Didn't you?' said Sheenah. She thought of Harold and felt again the grief of his rejection, quick and sharp. She thought of the burden of misery, and empathy began to instil itself insidiously into her mind. She did not want it there but it came anyway. A cold-blooded cat rustler this boy might be, but he was also a victim of the bewilderment and cowardice that besets existence.

'No,' said Steve. 'My mother refused to tell me anything about him. In fact she insisted I was the son of Lugh.'

'I can see that would be confusing.'

She walked over to the window and gazed out on to the dark garden below. The light from the kitchen shone on to the bird table as if it was a small stage, and as she leaned her forehead on the cold glass she looked down at the floor and saw a bundle of herbs wrapped in Granny Maldwyn's antique lace handkerchief. It was the Protection Spell that had disappeared from the kitchen door.

She picked it up and turned back into the room. 'Was it you who broke in and stole Catty from my house?'

'Yes,' said Steve.

'By hypnotising her, I suppose. You got that from your father.'

'Really? I just read a book and found I could do it.'

Sheenah was off before she could help herself.

'I met him in the circus. He was the Great Haroldo, hypnotising people as a trick, making them pretend to be bees and things. I was there visiting a friend, Gypsy Carmen Lee. (She wasn't a gypsy at all, actually, she was the daughter of a washing machine salesman from Nottingham.) Anyway, we fell in love and moved to London and he took up hypnotherapy. He was brilliant at it. People who had been addicted to nicotine for years came to see him. He could make people dying of emphysema give up. Everything. He had real talent.'

Steve was hopelessly interested. He wanted to listen all night, but there were other affairs to be addressed.

'I'm so sorry,' he said. 'I don't know what came over me. It's just that my mother is a domineering woman and very dangerous when aggravated. I thought she wanted to enhance a career spell. I had no idea she was practising black magic.'

'Well,' said Sheenah, who felt entitled to an act of contrition, despite the fact that he had Harold's eyes and despite the fact that it was one's moral duty to feel sorry for anyone who had the misfortune to be related by blood to Myra. 'The Coven of Covens will have to be informed, and I suggest that you're the best person to do it.'

'Mother's revenge will be terrible.'

'It's a risk you're going to have to take.'

A frown creased her brow and she inclined her head towards the door.

'What's that?' she said. 'Damn. I think I left the front door open.'

The sound of shuffling footsteps could be heard on the floorboards of the hallway.

154

The office door moved slowly inwards.

They both stared at it.

Three whiskers appeared followed by a furry face whose features were twisted by anger and fatigue.

'Catty!' shrieked Sheenah. 'Catty! Catty! Catty!'

Affectionate display was not in Catty's behavioural repertoire, but she did do the witch the favour of brushing past her legs a couple of times while her back was inspected for stab wounds.

'How on earth did she get here from Clapham?' said Steve.

'Catty, thanks to the grace of the Goddess Bast, happens to be very intelligent,' said Sheenah. 'Poor Catty.'

Talented though Catty was, science had failed to make the breakthrough required to award her with the gift of speech, so she was unable to inform them that she had caught the number forty-nine bus.

CHAPTER TWENTY-FOUR

It was important to obstruct Myra before she had time to rally, and rally she would. Steve was familiar with the obdurate fanaticism that bubbled inside her. The effects of being punched out by son and cat would not stall her, they would stimulate seismic rage. She would retaliate in a frenzy of fury: every hour of every day would be devoted to insuring the success of her own campaign and the merciless pulverisation of Sheenah. Lammas was less than a month away. Immediate and militant action was imperative.

Steve rang Angerboda's house in Somerset and was told by her granddaughter Frigga that she could be found at a New Age Festival in Walthamstow Town Hall. He drove his van dangerously fast down the Ml to Chigwell, past Chingford Hatch and along the North Circular.

The New Age Festival, which had received publicity on television, had attracted a much larger crowd than the organisers had expected. People crushed against each other as they attempted to find Kirlian photographers and reflexologists, faith healers and readers of the rainbow spectrum.

There were pendulums and posters, ionisers and oils, door chimes and greetings cards. There were sesame seed buns, Psyllium husks and sandwiches made out of falafel. Hundreds of incense sticks burned contemporaneously so that a haze floated below the ceiling and the room exuded a combination of sandalwood and myrrh superimposed by patchouli. This smell dominated because it was also worn on the bodies of the stall-holders, many of whom had never thrown away their Forbidden Fruit dresses and could be seen carrying slack shoulder bags decorated with small mirrors.

A man wearing an Afghan coat was painting psychedelic pictures on an easel. 'Zahoor the Trance Artist' said the notice in front of him. On the other side a blonde girl with black lips and a pierced nose was selling subliminal tapes with titles like, 'Flat Stomach' and 'Personality Dynamics'. Both stall-holders were smoking Lamberts and enjoying a throaty dialogue about the organisation of the New Age Festival which, they told each other, left a lot to be desired. The hall was not designed for a crowd of 550 people. That much was obvious to a blind person. Furthermore, the seminars were a joke. The Church of Scientology had been booked into the lecture hall at the same time as the Angry Pagan League.

An unseemly tussle had ensued as a result of this administrative error, and Steve's journey down the corridor was blocked by groups of wild-eyed 'clears' waving books about dianetics at hirsute pantheists wearing pieces of wood on leather thongs.

Pushing his way through the melange, Steve spotted a corner that had been shrouded with black velvet curtains and decorated with pictures of the bigger and more bearded Nordic deities. 'The Oracle of Odin' read the sign over the entrance. 'Angerboda, Queen of the Witches and High Priestess of the Coven of Covens, gives Accurate Clairvoyant Readings by Casting and Interpreting the Ancient European Rune Stones – £10.'

Freya was supposed to sit outside this makeshift tent to record Angerboda's appointments and take the money from clients, but, attracted by the noise of the confrontation in the corridor, she had slipped away to observe the fight.

Steve peered through the gap in the curtains.

'I'll be with you in a minute,' said Angerboda without looking up.

Hunched in this small cloth vestibule, she was glaring at an irregular conglomerate of wooden squares carved with diamonds and swastikas.

'Yes,' she finally said, 'I can feel you need help.'

'Er, Angerboda, Runic Mistress and Queen of the Witches, Matriarch and Leader of the Coven of Covens,' said Steve nervously. He was not sure of the protocol required by the presence of monarchy. 'I haven't come for a reading. I'm sorry to barge in and take up your valuable time like this, but I have something important to tell you.'

The Queen of the Witches sat erect, and her blue eyes did not blink. Her long grey hair was pulled neatly away from a calm, unlined face and she was possessed of a graceful deportment that emphasised her height and majesty. She seemed like someone who was about to ride from the north in a chariot in order to lay waste to the more peaceful and richer people of the south.

He swallowed.

The silence of the august personage was not encouraging.

'This is very difficult for me,' he said. 'I am Cu Cuchulainn, known as Steve, the son of Myra, Clan Mistress and Wiccan Mother of the South London Sisters of Diana.'

'Oh, yes,' said Angerboda. 'I met you once when you were five. You won't remember.'

Steve didn't.

The Queen scrutinised him. 'You've grown.'

Angerboda was tired. It had been a long day and she had been exposed to many hours of unvarying domestic problems.

'I've always liked Myra,' she said. 'She is a very unusual woman and it looks as if she will lead the Coven of Covens. I can't say it's not a relief. It's a very taxing job and I'm beginning to feel old despite the red clover tea and ginseng. I hope she's not ill.'

Steve narrated the heinous details that she needed to hear. Angerboda was horrified.

'This is very serious. Very serious indeed.' Her voice was low and shaking. 'Myra is so famous now. If it gets into the press we could have terrible trouble on our hands. The Coven of Covens could be forced underground again.'

'I know,' said Steve. 'What do you want to do?'

'There are suggestions outlined in *The Very Moste Secrete Booke of Witchery*,' said Angerboda. 'She will have to be disqualified, but I must consult the Chapter of the Lore to ascertain the correct procedure. I don't think anything like this has happened since Lilith the Bad was arrested for arson. In 1916, that was.'

The Queen of the Witches was upset. She had trusted Myra and now she had been tricked by her. Despite reigning for twenty long years as the Wisest Woman in the United Kingdom and Ireland (North and South), despite a series of globally acclaimed books about the mysteries of the runes, innumerable interviews, lectures and honours, her teenage granddaughters knew more than she. Angerboda felt miserable, humiliated, and very foolish.

She threw the runes on to the table. At least, in her experience, the symbols of the old ones had never lied.

'These will tell us what to do in the immediate future,' she said. 'Mmm.' She peered at a cross. 'Naut in Ing. That is a warning that our problems must be dealt with patiently. And the Thorn in Earth – aggravating another will cause her to lash out. Secrecy is our best course. Don't in the name of Odin's missing eye let your mother know you've been to see me. Avoid her if possible.'

'Okay.'

Freya poked her head through the curtain. 'Granny?' she said. Then she saw the figure in the leather jacket. 'Oh, sorry. I thought you were alone.'

'It's all right,' said Angerboda. 'We've finished.'

'A client is here.'

Steve left.

'Who was that stunning man?' whispered Freya.

'Trouble,' said Angerboda.

159

CHAPTER TWENTY-FIVE

Steve was correct about his mother's reaction to attempts to impede her progress. A dislocated shoulder, bruised spine and minor cuts served as stimuli to retaliation rather than capitulation. Preliminary scuffles are traditional in open confrontation, and Myra entered the combat zone with the speed and efficiency of one who is confident of her superior position.

On the Monday following the undignified dust-up in her Black Temple, she filed a doctor's report with her lawyer and instructed him to look into the possibility of bringing a civil action against her son. Then she hired a security firm who advised her to change all the locks and replace them with sophisticated combination devices that could only be opened with cards carried by people who had been individually vetted and cleared. This accomplished, she purchased a bullet-proof limousine and put it on her BBC expense account. Protection thus acquired, she called a summit meeting of all campaign staff.

The countenances of the Daughters of Calatin and Sisters of Diana were serious as they sat down. The sight of locksmiths kneeling in doorways, and men with walkie-talkies standing on the roof had given rise to the rumour that there had been an assassination attempt.

At 11.43 am the candidate hobbled in. She was wearing dark glasses and a yellow suit by Ungaro. Her right arm was in a sling and her left hand gripped a walking stick on top of which was an elaborately carved silver knob.

She was followed, at a respectful distance, by two enormous cyborgs who were also wearing dark glasses. As they proceeded forward, they pushed invisible objects out of the way with fists the size of marble plinths, and they stared belligerently at the assembly as if every one of them was standing on a grassy knoll. One sat in a chair behind the High Priestess and the other stood looking out of the window for evidence of drive-by shooters. As he flicked the curtain with ostentatious care the holster that carried his automatic weapon could be seen by all.

The campaign staff, silent, rustled their papers, and wondered who was destined to suffer for obligations unfulfilled.

Myra did not impart the details of the violence that had been administered to her person but concentrated on the flaws that had appeared in the campaign strategy. Eumonia, leader of the Daughters of Calatin, reported the election was in the balance because the endorsement of the Folkstone Faeries had still not been pledged to either party.

Myra slowly, nonchalantly, removed her dark glasses and with a look that could have felled an ox at a distance of two hundred yards said:

'Daphne of the Sisters of Diana, I believe you are the coordinating officer for Folkstone.'

Daphne saw her life pass in front of her eyes.

'I thought Folkstone was in the bag,' she stammered. 'Belladonna has no television, no telephone, no car and no credit card. She doesn't even have a bank account. Nothing. It was very difficult to obtain information about her, but eventually I tracked down the High Priest and he told me that she planned to vote for you even though the rest of the Faeries are evenly divided. I assumed we were okay.'

'There is no room for any assumptions in circumstances such as these,' Myra snapped icily. 'I would fire you for laziness, stupidity and incompetence, Daphne of the Sisters of Diana. Given half a chance, I would excommunicate you from the Coven itself. But I need your expertise. You know, or should know, more about this sector than anybody.'

Myra stood up and a bodyguard stood up at the same time. The terrible force of her anger settled like frost. 'From now on,' she said, 'I want you all to concentrate on *Operation Nobble the Faeries*. I want to know everything about this coven. Who they are, where they meet, what they eat for their bloody dinner. I want their filthy biographical details and I want

161

them by the end of today. This meeting will reconvene at six pm. That is all.'

She hobbled out, and after checking underneath seats and tables for bugs and/or explosive devices the two frightening lunkheads followed her.

The twenty-two members of the campaign team worked through lunch and by six o'clock a disturbing fact had come to light. Belladonna, it seemed, was under the influence of the High Priest who was (he had failed to admit to Daphne) an avid supporter of Sheenah.

'And what, pray,' said Myra, 'do we know about this misguided member of the male sex?'

'He's a GP.'

'And is his a coven devoted to the pleasures of skyclad ritual?' inquired Myra softly.

She could feel the gleam of the mighty Choronzon's eyes shining upon her.

The Masters of Darkness had not let her down.

'Yes, they are,' said Daphne, looking down at her notes. 'They were actually founded by a Gardnerian witch who used to live on the Isle of Man.'

Myra laughed uproariously. 'Well! There you are! It couldn't be more simple!'

Daphne blinked at her. The bewildered expression on her face reflected that the subtext of this plot had escaped her.

'Oh, really, Daphne!' snapped Myra. 'Do I have to explain fucking everything? Keep up! Sometimes I think you've been supplied without batteries. The good medicine man is not going to want everybody to know that he flounces around naked in the light of the full moon, is he? Go down to Folkstone at the next esbat and take photographs.'

'Me?'

'Yes, Daphne of the Sisters of Diana, *you*.'

Daphne of the Sisters of Diana was an aromatherapist by profession and had only taken this job because her husband had been made redundant and they were behind with their mortgage payments. She was not qualified, either emotionally or professionally, to lurk around in the darkness of Folkstone taking photographs of nude doctors. She was beginning to wish that Myra *had* fired and excommunicated her.

162

However, as we know, the potential of the average human being usually remains untested. Daphne of the Sisters of Diana drove her husband's unpaid-for Datsun to Folkstone and performed the deed, undetected, thanks to a helpful sand dune (the Faeries performed their ceremonies on the beach).

Myra was furnished with clear colour photographs of the undressed physician with his lips enthusiastically planted on the puckered breast of Belladonna, who was holding a wand in one hand and a whip in the other. This, to witches, was merely the sight of a High Priest performing the 'Fivefold Kiss' which precedes the Charge to the Goddess and is a part of every Opening Ritual. It is accompanied by the words, 'Blessed be thy breasts, formed in beauty', and is central to a sacred ceremony devoted to the worship of the Divine Feminine, She Who Sees All.

To those ignorant of the Wiccan Way it was a permissive display (with sado-masochist overtones) of a respected member of the community whose job demanded behavioural decorum.

The lurid snaps were dispatched immediately, accompanied by a note (on scented paper) from Myra, saying that they had been sent to her by mistake, but it was their little secret . . . wasn't it?

A day later a fax came through to the campaign office informing the candidate that the coven known as the Faeries of Folkstone was not only unanimous in their declaration of support for Myra but they had signed an oath in blood.

Operation Nobble the Faeries having been successfully discharged, Myra turned her attentions to those dissident Elders whose allegiance to Sheenah seemed to be irrevocable. Although the endorsement of Folkstone put her in the lead, it was only one vote and Myra did not want a marginal victory. She wanted a landslide.

In order to avoid attracting unnecessary suspicion Myra told her campaign team to leave Dublin and Carlisle alone. They had nominated two outsiders, but if these independent runners did not receive the support of their own delegates difficult questions might be asked.

East London (the Norns) and Cambridge (the House of Phoebe) quickly succumbed to financial persuasion – a tactic

Myra preferred to bargaining with policy concessions. Cardiff (the Daughters of Branwen) proved less easy to influence, for loyalty to the memory of Granny Maldwyn united them with an adamantine obstinacy. Then there was a communications breakthrough. The youngest member of the coven turned out to be the anonymous organiser of the lesbian animal rights group known as Bitches on Heat. Devoted to a policy of guerrilla tactics and unashamed violence, these activists had, according to underground informants, been responsible for blowing up a battery farmer outside Aberystwyth.

The Masters of the Underworld had come through again.

The Daughters of Branwen changed sides.

The only Elders impervious to the unrestrained tactics of Myra's political machine were Merlin (her senior aides advised against attempting to canvass him) and, unexpectedly, Charles, the leader of the all-male coven known as Thor's Hammer, who represented the witches of Scotland.

Myra dispatched her secret weapon in the form of Selene. Selene, the Handmaiden of the Daughters of Calatin, was an unemployed actress blessed with dazzling beauty. She had sleek auburn hair, huge breasts and glossed lips.

She was sent to Edinburgh with instructions to discompose the great Wise Man by seducing him. Once overwhelmed, the plan was to fill his mind with stories that reflected the callous nature of Sheenah's personality and subtly persuade him to vote for Myra.

The Scots Elder, unfortunately, managed to combine an adherence to Catholicism with his pagan path and applied a dogmatic fidelity to the papal edict that there should be no sex before marriage. He remained cordially oblivious to the imaginative series of carnal temptations offered by Selene.

Undaunted by this news, Myra bade Selene to attempt to sleep with the rest of Thor's Hammer. They couldn't all, she said, be the celibate victims of religious mania. After negotiating a seventy-five per cent pay rise, Selene agreed.

But time was running out. Even Selene, a woman of pneumatic skill and experience, was daunted by the challenge of sleeping with all twelve of Thor's Hammer in ten days. She was not, as she complained to Eumonia in a reverse charge call made from a public telephone box in Princes Street, 'Bloody Messalina'.

'Never mind,' Eumonia sympathised. 'At least when this is over you can go and lie in the sun in Bermuda.'

'No thanks,' grumbled Selene. 'I'll have had quite enough of being on my back.'

Myra was not particularly worried. It would have been rewarding for reasons of revenge to lure Thor's Hammer to her side, but she was confident of a safe majority.

The crown was hers.

Choronzon and the Masters of the Inferno had vanquished her opponents. Soon She and They would be girded by the revelations of *The Very Moste Secrete Booke of Witchery*, not to mention the six million pounds in the Sacred Bank Account.

Just as many tourists are relieved that their coach trip avoids the Gaza Strip, so Steve was delighted that Angerboda had commanded him to steer a course around his mother. He enjoyed a week in which a relaxing silence was unbroken by shrill beratement.

Certain that his heresies would be repaid with pitiless magickal reprisals, Steve regularly checked his temperature to ensure that he was not the victim of the Curse of Poisoned Blood and looked in the mirror for signs of the Punishment of Polyp and Pustule. His skin and health remained intact, but he could not stop his mind from entertaining the horrors of recrimination that would, he knew, hover over his life. So when he received a letter from his mother's lawyer stating her intention to sue him for two million pounds for 'assault and battery', it was something of a release. At least now there was less worry about the telepathic transference of gland enlargement. At least now Steve had palpable evidence of what she was planning.

The day after the arrival of this communiqué the telephone rang, and when he had eventually located it in a pool of oil underneath the rusting chassis of an old Mustang Steve answered it.

'Yes?' he said, wiping his hands down the front of his overalls and transferring the apparatus to a less stained corner of his workshop.

'Is that Cu Cuchulainn, Son of Myra of the South London Sisters of Diana?' inquired an unfamiliar female tone.

'Steve. Yes.'

'This is Freya, granddaughter of Angerboda, Queen of the Witches, Ultimate Degree Initiate and Ruler of the Covens of England, Ireland, Scotland and Wales.' She paused to regain her breath. 'Her Majesty would like a word.'

'Of course.'

This was followed by a lengthy and noiseless interval. Steve assumed that Angerboda was easing herself towards the telephone from the other end of a very long house. In fact Freya was clinging to the receiver like a barnacle attempting to make up her mind as to whether to pursue the possibility of a date. Eventually her grandmother wrested the phone from her grasp.

'Cuchulainn, Hound of Ulster?'

Angerboda's voice echoed down the line.

'Steve. Yes.'

Angerboda's telephone manner was loud and slow, as if she was conversing with somebody on a bad line from Rawalpindi.

'Cuchulainn, Son of Myra, I have consulted *The Very Moste Secrete Booke of Witchery* with reference to the matters we discussed, and I find that the situation is more complicated than I had originally envisaged.'

'Oh, yes?'

'The Chapter of the Lore which pertains to iniquity such as this was written by the Secret Chiefs in the seventeenth century when thousands of innocent people were sentenced to death, despite inadequate proof and farcical trials . . .'

'Yes.'

'Consequently the Rules outlined in the Chapter of the Lore are protective of those who might have been wrongly accused. The Lore demands that visible and tangible evidence must be supplied in cases where candidates are accused of a relationship with the Devil. Not only this, but the visible and tangible proof has to be examined and considered genuine by every member of the Coven of Covens before the accused can be officially disqualified in a Sacred Ceremony of Eternal Repulsion. Your word, the word of a son, is not enough. During the pain and hysteria of the Burning Times, you see, many families were tortured into accusing each other.'

'What does visible and tangible evidence mean?' asked Steve.

'I suppose we need to see an object connected with the Invocation of the Infernal Beasts – a chalice of blood, say, an inverted pentacle or a symbol of the Judas Goat. *The Very Moste Secrete Booke of Witchery* defines black magic as' (Angerboda read from the notes she had taken while sitting in the vault at the Bank of England) ' "the Performance of Magickal Ceremonies to Communicate with the Forces of Devilry that they might commit evil and cruele discharge." So it's up to us to interpret as we judge best.'

Steve pondered upon these illuminations and attempted unsuccessfully to conjure a practical counter-manoeuvre, for he was keen to compensate for the fact that these disasters were due to his own moral flaccidity.

'What do you suggest?' he said, hoping that the omniscient runic offerings of the Wise Old Wiccan would have supplied her with a cunning scheme.

'I'm stumped, to tell you the truth,' Angerboda said. 'There are only seven working days until the election. My granddaughter Freya informs me that Myra has received the pledge of Folkstone, and looks set to land East London and Cambridge. Even without my vote, she will win. I am praying to the Goddess for advice and sustenance, but I am increasingly afraid that, after all these aeons, the Coven of Covens has become the victim of Mother Nature's sense of humour. When She invented the survival of the fittest She must have known it would encourage violence and greed.'

'Let me think about it,' said Steve. 'I'll see if I can come up with anything that might be of help.'

'I'd appreciate it,' said the poor old Queen. 'I'm desperate.'

He felt like going to the pub and drinking a pint of Old Peculiar, but he didn't. He slammed his van round to Eaton Terrace.

There was the usual gaggle of motorcycle messengers, florists, visagistes and dukes waiting to be granted an audience.

Ivy quick-stepped to a position just below his nose.

'Miss Arundell is in her bedroom.'

'Is she decent?'

'She's deciding what to wear to Balmoral,' was the succinct report. 'I don't know whether you'd call that decent or not.'

Rosaleen's bedroom looked like a natural disaster area. Every surface was hidden underneath mounds of multitextured, multicoloured vestments of varying sizes, styles, eras and quality. The floor was a carpet of satin stilettos, leather pumps, walking shoes, riding boots, wellington boots and exotic designs of unidentifiable function. Polythene bags full of ball dresses lay as if they had fainted over the chaise longue 'day bed'. Hangers bearing Harris tweed jackets balanced on the top of picture frames, doorknobs were camouflaged by riding hats and, on the dressing table, sprawled a spaghetti junction of necklaces, earrings, chokers, riding gloves and hair nets.

Finally, on what was safe to assume was the bed, there were hundreds and hundreds of kilts. From somewhere underneath this chequered Chogo Ri there came a movement, much like a skink rustling through the undergrowth.

Rosaleen's head popped up from the area dominated by the red and green conjunction that are the colours of the McGregor clan.

'Oh, hullo,' she said, throwing a velvet hairband to one side.

'You're busy.'

'Yes. It's only a weekend, but you have to change seventeen times a day. Ivy's been trying to get through to the lady-in-waiting for precise instruction as to what to wear and when to walk backwards, but they're all in Marbella with King Juan Carlos.'

'Oh.'

'Why haven't you rung?' Rosaleen said, hoping that the timbre of her voice sounded nonchalant.

Steve didn't answer, but concentrated on sweeping a clearing for himself on the chaise longue. Then he noticed the rose quartz by the fireplace.

'Christ on a bike!' he cried. 'What's that?'

Rosaleen explained that she had bought it in order to invigorate the love spell they had been taught by Sheenah.

168

'Then no wonder there's so much chaos in this house,' Steve said. 'It's much too big, Rosaleen. You should get rid of it, or at the very least take it out of the bedroom. I'm surprised you can sleep at all. I'm surprised you haven't been *raped*. Love magick is supposed to be worked with little incy crystals, not a great boulder like this. You don't know what you're dealing with. It could be very dangerous.'

Rosaleen fell silent. She had come to depend on the miracles of the pink talisman – its influence had revolutionised her life. She credited it with the esteem in which she was now held by urbane London and for the banquets to which she was invited. Exhausted though she was by chronic conviviality, receiving the love of the world was more attractive than the idea of returning to a life in which dates were only attended by herself and a boiled egg.

Then she realised that if she had to relinquish the numinous love aid, then she had better inflame Steve before she did so.

Lurching her shoulders back and her breasts fiercely forward, Rosaleen plummeted on to the chaise longue next to Steve. Then she studied him through eyelids whose nictating activity made them look as if they were searching for a suitable floor on which to tap dance.

She kicked off her shoes.

One smashed against a photograph of her mother; the other missed Steve's head by inches.

Rosaleen wriggled.

She breathed.

She removed her Aran cardigan.

She looked as if she was being poked by an invisible stick.

'Is something wrong?' Steve eventually inquired.

'Oh, for God's sake,' she said, as if he had just made a poor decision in the middle of a game of bridge. 'I'm waiting for you to ravish me.'

'Good heavens,' Steve said, his face aglow with an uncomfortable blush.

'What?' lisped the sapid temptress.

'Good heavens.'

'What?'

'I'm married.'

There was a very long silence. The blood rushed into Rosaleen's ears, making a noise similar to the surf off Miami Beach.

'You're . . .' She cleared her throat, for it seemed to have become blocked by a large object. 'You're what?'

'Married. I'm married. My wife is seven months pregnant. That's why I allowed my mother to bribe me so easily. It was unplanned, you see, and we were desperately short of money. She's called Jean.'

'Jean? Jean!'

Rosaleen fell back fanning her face with her hand. She had never met anyone called Jean before, but then she had never been to Gibraltar and she had no doubt that it existed.

Jean.

She flailed around for an appropriate response to this Christian name that had crash-landed into her bedroom, then she blurted out, 'You led me on!'

'No, I didn't, Rosaleen,' he said gently. 'I never led you on.'

She reconstructed the episodes of their acquaintance and she had to admit that this was true. She had led herself on. She was the victim of her own fevered mental ramblings. She had thought he was playing an interesting game of detachment in order to entice her when he hadn't been at all. He had been married.

'What about that hug?'

'Oh, Rosaleen!' He spoke with the sadness of one who wonders if it is he who is handicapped by inadequate intelligence, or whether it is others who need to retain a more tenacious grip on reality. 'I thought you were my friend and I needed a friend who understood about this witchcraft nonsense. If I slept with all my friends I'd be exhausted and my marriage would fall to pieces.'

'I see.'

Silence.

'Why don't you wear a ring?' Or, she wanted to add, a sandwich board saying 'Property of Jean'.

'It gets in the way when I'm welding. I wear it around my neck. Look.'

He parted his shirt, like curtains, in order to provide inescapable evidence of this custom. As she examined the gold

170

band, Rosaleen saw something that made the heartache of rejection and the pain of unrequited ardour slightly easier to manage.

Steve had a hairy chest.

She did not, as was her instinct, leap back as if she had been scorched, but she felt much calmer and her breathing returned to normal.

They moved on quickly, like stand-up comedians who have realised that the audience is not amused.

Steve revealed the latest episode in the run-up to the election. Myra's popularity was increasing and she would become Queen unless evidence of her perfidy was produced. He told Rosaleen about his telephone conversation with Angerboda.

Rosaleen shared the Queen's opinion. There seemed little to be done. Then her eye caught the rose crystal.

'We could give Myra the quartz,' she said. 'Perhaps it would neutralise the energy or something.'

It was a half-hearted suggestion made casually, but Steve leaped to his feet shouting:

'That is *brilliant*! Totally BRILLIANT! That's exactly what we've got to do. I doubt even a crystal like this would be powerful enough to stop her completely, but it would certainly make black magic more difficult to perform. But how do we plant it on her? She's changed all the locks so my key is useless, and the place is overrun by some kind of goon squad.'

Rosaleen considered this. 'Does she have a garden?' she asked.

'Yes. Quite big. At the back.'

'I'll ring Gerald Huckaback,' she said. 'He's got a helicopter. We might not be able to put the crystal in the house, but there's nothing to stop us winching it into the garden.'

'Unless she has anti-aircraft guns on the roof.'

'Huckaback won't mind that. He's a lunatic.'

Rosaleen watched as he buttoned his shirt over the woolly woof of his thorax, then she walked calmly towards the telephone.

It could never have worked.

CHAPTER TWENTY-SIX

Sheenah did not fully comprehend why so many of her long-term supporters were defecting, but she was aware that she was the victim of a dirty-tricks campaign. The underhand nature of Myra's operation made it insuperable – it would have been easier to oppose overt vituperation.

Even allowing for the vagaries of the electorate's opinion, the apostasy of the Daughters of Branwen was inexplicable. A coven of moderates and traditionalists whose allegiance to Sheenah was unanimous, their Elder, Mathonwy, had often spoken of Myra's vulgarity and had even written a leader column in *Wicca Weekly* saying that an administration led by her would debase the honour of the fine ways of the Old Religion. The coven's secession was the final sign that, despite Merlin's courageous attempts to rally support, Sheenah's campaign was losing its grip.

It was time to provide the visible and tangible proof Steve had told her was required to support any allegation that Myra was practising black magic.

If diabolism was being performed in the temple at Clapham Common it was likely that animals were being maltreated. The use of blood to ingratiate oneself with Lucifuge Rocofocale goes back to the Grimoire of Pope Honorius the Great. And maybe further.

Sheenah asked Cuthbert if there was anything the RSPCA could do about it, and he said that although their legal powers were limited they often received reports of this nature and he would look into it immediately.

Myra was sitting at her Sheraton desk reading a script for her show. The house was quiet. She had dismissed the bodyguards because they kept bumping into the antiques. The campaign office was empty. Now that she was sure of success, only a part-time secretary was required.

The door bell rang and she heard Pallas Athene show somebody into the drawing room.

'Madam,' announced the girl, 'there's two gentlemen.'

'So? I told you I was working and didn't want to see anybody.'

'They're in uniforms, ma'am. They might be the filth, I mean the police.'

Sighing stertorously Myra stood up, slammed the script down on the desk and went to the window. A dark blue RSPCA van was parked in her driveway in full view of the whole of Clapham Common.

'Fuck,' she said. 'Give the gentlemen some tea and biscuits, Athene. Use the good china. I'll be down in a minute.'

Myra gathered herself up. She primped her dark hair and lacquered it into a helmet. She ensured that her make-up was convincing and smooth, and she sprayed a little Giorgio behind her ears. Then she slipped into a white silk Jean Muir skirt.

Her entrance into the drawing room was somewhere between the heroine of an opera (*Tosca*, perhaps, or *Norma*) and the kindly staff nurse of a national health hospital.

She saw two men in blue uniforms sitting on her George III parcel-gilt canapé. One was young with red hair, and one was older with a grey beard.

They were very sorry to disturb her, they said, but they had received some reports that animals were suffering and they were under obligation to look into the matter.

Myra, as her televisual successes had proved, was a natural model for that cloak of deception known as acting. Struggling to emphasise the fact that her arm (which was still in a sling) was causing her stabbing pain, she limped across the room and eased herself into an ornately gilded bergère opposite the two officials.

She looked very surprised and very hurt.

Cuthbert's supervising officer, whose name was Herbrand, was quite moved by this performance and felt they had unfairly infiltrated the home of a beautiful, famous and obviously innocent woman of taste.

173

In his opinion, women with curtains bound by huge knobbly silk cords did not murder cats. He began to develop a grudge against Cuthbertson, who had insisted that they did. It was things like this that made his job very difficult.

He leaned forward, thin porcelain cup dwarfed in a hand more suited to feeding drugged meat to furious Rottweilers, and said that he and the wife had seen her show on the television and that they thought it was very good, much better than that chap with the 'orrible 'airdo on the other side.

Myra nodded graciously.

Cuthbert, realising the interrogation was not propelling itself into the realms of hard fact, asked if he might go to the bathroom. Myra rang a small hand bell. Athene appeared, and Cuthbert was shown downstairs to the gents' cloakroom.

Exiting the ornate washroom, he opened a door opposite and found himself in what was obviously Myra's temple. He walked around, checking the details with the diligent, trained eye of a former constable. Nosing around the candles and dead flowers, he scraped his finger along surfaces and saw no signs of illegal activity. He was about to leave when he noticed that the drape behind the altar was pulled slightly to one side and there seemed to be some kind of cavity behind. If his nose did not deceive him, a smell of sulphur was emanating from it.

He squeezed through, dust spattering the RSPCA uniform, and found himself in a room that reminded him of a public urinal. There were drops of dried blood on the floor. On the coffin cover that had been thrown over the altar there was a picture of a demon with the horns of a goat and the face of a maniac, a bowl full of chicken heads into which rusting nails had been pushed and the lifeless body of a Mandarin duck, which Cuthbert Cuthbertson knew to be protected by law.

Trainee Inspector Cuthbertson took detailed photographs with the Kodak Flashy Whizz Mini-Matic his mother had given him for Christmas. Then, with shaking hands, he gathered up his evidence.

He returned to the fresh yellow atmosphere of the drawing room where the sunlight shone through sash windows on to Regency rosewood cabinets and occasional tables with barley-twist stems.

174

Myra, perched on the edge of her tightly upholstered chair, was turned away from him.

'What,' Cuthbert said in the casual but menacing tones he had implemented when arresting car thieves on the White City estate, 'are these?'

Myra mimed genuine surprise.

The porcelain cup rattled in the hand of Herbrand, and his mouth fell open like a pilfered handbag.

On a silver plate in Cuthbert's hand lay bloodstained beaks, congealed eyeballs and mangled feathers.

'I've never seen them before in my life,' said Myra calmly and with a plan already formulated in which Athene would take the blame. 'I don't know where you could have got them from.'

'You know very well where I got them from,' said Cuthbert sternly. 'I suggest you contact your lawyer.'

Unnoticed, outside in the garden, bathed in the violet glow that is claimed by experienced adepts to signify the astral light, the rose quartz shone beneath the rhododendron bush where Gerald Huckaback had successfully lowered it, on a pulley, from his chopper.

CHAPTER TWENTY-SEVEN

Lammas, or Lughnasadh, is a Celtic fire festival. Traditionally the ceremony is held outdoors.

The rites involved in the election and coronation of the Queen of the Witches had been outlined in immortal detail by the Secret Chiefs, and had not changed since the investiture of the first Queen (Lady Sophia) in 1610.

The Sabbat was held on top of the cliffs overlooking the sea at Lulworth Cove and because it was the most important day of the coven's year selected outsiders were invited to join in what Merlin referred to as a 'ginormous knees up'.

And so, as the ebbing light of the summer sun flickered over the sea below, the Elders of the Coven of Covens made their way over the plushy grasses of the cliffs towards the bonfire which, for some of them, symbolised the heat and anger of Lugh's nature. They wore dark robes in memory of antecedents who had been obliged to camouflage themselves, and also because the sea breeze that nipped about the cliffs could become sharp as the sun set.

They seated themselves in two circles around the fire. The Inner Circle, naturally, comprised the Elders; the Outer Circle was made up of guests and candidates. This evening it included Marilyn, Clan Mother of the Muses of Minehead, Dame Hebadonia of the Wild Hunt, Sheenah, Freya, Frigga, Cuthbert, Rosaleen, Steve and seven-month-pregnant Jean.

At the astrologically significant time of 8.13 pm, Angerboda rattled a tambourine, stood up and thumped the carved Electoral Staff on the ground. Then, as the sky faded to grisaille around her, and with her back towards the sea, she raised her arms in the air in a gesture of invocation. In tones that carried easily over the stage whisper of the sea and the shy

176

murmur of the wind through the grasses, she called to Lugh and Dana to look down upon them at this the time of the first fruits of harvest, and to grace their esbat with the wisdom and peace that befitted its noble intention.

Then she sat down upon the wooden throne that Merlin had heaved up the hill (along with a consecrated fire extinguisher in case of emergencies). There was silence, except for the occasional tortured yell of a seagull.

Angerboda opened the election with the following proclamation:

'I, Angerboda, Initiator of the Oracle of Odin, Queen of the Witches of England, Ireland, Scotland and Wales and Royal Sapience over all the covens therein, do hereby declare that at this Lammas-tide, as decreed by the Secret Chiefs, a new Queen will be chosen to lead the Wise People into the uncharted territory of the forthcoming year. By the powers vested in me by the statutes of *The Very Moste Secrete Booke of Witchery* I do hereby command the balloting to begin.'

A round of applause from the seated Inner Circle was customary at this juncture, but Angerboda thumped her staff quickly on the ground and waved her hand to emphasise that levity was inappropriate, for she was the bringer of sad tidings.

'It has come to my attention,' she said, 'that among the aspirants to Wiccan sovereignty there is one who has banefully ignored the most sacred rule in the Chapter of the Lore. Myra, Mistress of the South London Sisters of Diana, stands accused, O Coven of my Covens, of indulging in the forbidden practice of Black Magic.'

The Inner Circle sharply intook its breath.

'This practice, as ye well know, carries the forfeit of instant disqualification from the contest for Honourable Office of Queen. But so, too, is the accused entitled to a fair hearing.'

She gazed with her calm blue eyes at the faces of the Elders. Some registered guilt, some shock, some misery.

'Myra, of the South London Sisters of Diana, has chosen not to grace the Outer Circle with her presence,' said Angerboda. 'And this, in my humble opinion, is not the augury of innocence. However the Goddess knows how wrong I have been in the recent past, and the Constitution of the Coven of Covens demands that visible and tangible evidence is required to prove that these execrable rituals have been executed. You, as Elders, are ordained with the responsibility of passing judgement on Myra.'

She signalled to Cuthbert, who sprang from his cross-legged position in the Outer Circle and, red-hair static with excitement, handed her a series of Mini-Matic colour photographs.

'I took pictures of the chicken heads and the duck as well because they were getting a bit, you know . . . ' He pulled a face to communicate the more revolting stages of decomposition. 'You couldn't really transport them because of the smell and flies and . . . '

'Quite,' said Angerboda. 'Thank you, Initiate Cuthbertson, for your help in this terrible business.'

'That's okay, your Maj,' he said, grinning with a little less formality than is customary in the presence of exalted personages.

The incarnadine images of murder were passed from hand to hand around the Inner Circle.

As she gazed at the gore and grume that were the dregs of feathered life, Belladonna thought she might faint.

Merlin caught Levanah's eye and the Dark Woman of Knowledge smiled grimly back at him.

Bridget of the Oracle of Queen Maeve was subsumed with guilt and resolved to give every penny she made from the sales of *Which Witch is Which?* to the RSPCA in order to balance her karma as quickly as possible.

Charles of Thor's Hammer wondered if all this had anything to do with the extraordinary wee lassie who wore so few clothes and kept jumping out at members of his coven.

The photographs returned to the hands of Angerboda.

She thumped the Electoral Staff.

'If the Accused is found guilty of Communing with the Devile for Cruel and Evil Discharge,' she announced in a sepulchral monotone, 'she will be subject to the Sacred Ceremony of Eternal Repulsion.

'Now I ask you, O Wise Ones of the Higher Echelons of the Craft, to decide on the fate of the plaintiff. Those who find Myra not guilty raise their hands.'

Everyone looked at each other.

The sun glowered red and dipped on to the edge of the horizon.

A tear shone in Belladonna's eye.

No arm was raised.

'Guilty?' shouted Angerboda.

Slowly, quietly, with unhappy solemnity, all arms lifted into the air.

Angerboda threw some purifying incense on to the bonfire. It puffed into a blue-grey cirrus then dived back into the flames.

'I hereby confer on Myra, traitorous witch of Clapham, the sacred forfeit of Eternal Repulsion. Thus she shall be banned from the realms of witchery. No coven shall allow her among its number, no witch shall speak with her, no child of the Craft of the Wise shall listen to her words lest her tongue be forked. Myra of South London, who hath cast her dark light upon all our struggling souls, is in exile for all incarnations.'

She banged the Electoral Staff on the ground and wrote Myra's name on a blank sheet in *The Very Moste Secret Booke of Witchery*. Tearing the page out and holding it up for all to see, she flung it angrily into the flames.

'I smite thy name from the Coven of Covens for Eternal Time. So mote it be.'

'So mote it be,' mumbled the subdued assembly.

'*Absit Omen.*'

'*Absit Omen.*'

Everybody watched the flames lick the yellow parchment. Soon it turned black and the name of Myra was consumed.

Sheenah silently thanked the Goddess for showing balance and judgement and prayed that she would not, at the last moment, with terrible perversity, favour Dame Hebadonia. She looked down at her newly painted nails (silver) and her wedding ring, and flicked an ant off her royal blue jersey dress. It had been a difficult sartorial decision, the dress. She and Merlin had spent hours discussing it. (Merlin always enjoyed a debate about clothes.) One did not want to look as if one expected to be Queen, but neither did one want to be unstylishly clad in the event of being voted in. She noted with relief that Dame Hebadonia and Marilyn were obviously of a similar opinion. Dame Hebadonia's bob had recently received a cerise rinse, and Marilyn was wearing an immaculate corduroy trouser suit.

'And now,' said Angerboda, 'we may proceed with the casting of the votes.'

The ballot box was passed around and each witch placed a slip of paper in the slot at the top of it. As Angerboda slowly counted them out the atmosphere around the fire shifted from one of shocked dejection to discreet excitement, which escalated in intensity as the reigning monarch unfolded each piece of paper.

Merlin winked at Sheenah.

Cuthbert poked Rosaleen in the arm.

Dame Hebadonia looked under her cushion to make sure there were no slugs.

Steve stared into the fire.

Seven-month-pregnant Jean smiled with earth-mother beatitude.

The moon appeared in the sky. A full, confident orb, its pale effluence streaked the black sea as it had done on this night of Lammas for hundreds of years.

Angerboda stood up.

She beat the Electoral Staff (unnecessarily) for silence.

'I have great pleasure in announcing that the new Queen of the Witches is Sheenah, High Priestess of the Divine Order of Isis.'

The tension snapped.

Everybody leaped to their feet and screamed.

Charles of Thor's Hammer gave Belladonna a fireman's lift.

Cuthbert hugged Rosaleen.

Steve pecked her on the cheek.

Seven-month-pregnant Jean smiled with earth-mother beatitude.

Sheenah was pushed and pulled by grabbing hands until she found herself in front of the throne where Angerboda welcomed her with a wide smile and embraced her.

'Congratulations, dear,' she whispered. 'You deserve it, you really do.'

Sheenah knelt down, head bowed.

Angerboda placed the sash of majesty over her head, handed her *The Very Moste Secrete Booke of Witchery* and bade her read the Oath of Guardianship. Then the proud Rune-Mistress, her reign finally over, took the triple-pointed crown from her own head and placed it on Sheenah's.

'I name thee Queen of the Witches.'

The clamour of cheering and clapping resounded around the cliffs, bounced off the ancient granite and echoed to the beach below where it mingled with the sibilance of the rolling waves.

Sheenah, new Queen of the Witches, sat down on the throne and, with the triple-pointed crown of imperial authority sitting heavily upon her head, she struggled against a wave of dream-like incredulity.

There was a brief lull in the wild approbation. She wondered, fleetingly, if she would be able to cope with the responsibilities of office, but this thought evaporated under the self-confidence that is sometimes the by-product of uncontrollable circumstance.

'Thank you,' she said, blushing. 'I'll do my best.'

Then a lyre was plugged into an amplifier. Potatoes, sausages and chicken legs were thrown on the fire. Plastic containers of coleslaw appeared, and a frothing harvest mead was poured into eagerly proffered tankards. The Elders of the Coven of Covens and their guests proceeded (with the exception of Jean) to become giddy and muddled.

Rosaleen found herself whirled about by Merlin in a loose interpretation of a waltz. Eventually disorientated by the blood swirling about their craniums, they collapsed on to the grass that had been flattened by stamping feet.

'So,' said Merlin, replenishing Rosaleen's tankard, 'did you get a boyfriend after all that?'

Rosaleen smiled. 'I got hundreds, actually, but no one – you know – serious.'

'Oh.' He looked disappointed. 'But it was worth it, though, doing the evening classes?'

'Oh, yes,' she said.

'At least you didn't end up falling for some hairy-chested married person,' he said.

Astonished by the accuracy of the wizard's extrasensory perception and the enormity of his magical powers, Rosaleen's jaw dropped.

Merlin smiled back enigmatically, and his eyes followed hers as she stared at Steve who was standing near the dying bonfire. Steve said something to Sheenah. The Queen nodded and patted him on the shoulder with the hand that was not clasping *The Very Moste Secrete Booke of Witchery* and an empty tankard. Then he turned and, waving goodbye, guided the seven-month-pregnant (and now tired) Jean across the cliffs to where the van was parked.

Sheenah walked over to Merlin and Rosaleen, her deportment unnaturally erect and her gait slow due to the pressure of the crown.

'Pleased?' asked Merlin.

'Yes,' she said, 'of course. But . . . ' Her voice trailed off.

'Mmm?'

'I can't help wishing Harold was here. I was just talking to Steve about him. It's a shame, really.'

Merlin was slightly affronted. Women! You did everything you could for them, and they still hankered after some bald git they hadn't seen for twenty-five years. And Sheenah, he observed to himself, had been remarkably quick to forgive the person who had broken into her house and kidnapped her Catty.

'Oh, Harold,' he said, impatiently waving his hand in a dismissive gesture. 'Harold, Harold, Harold. He was nothing but trouble.'

Sheenah stared out to the full moon, the blanket of stars and the black sea. She seemed not to hear.

'He has a grandchild on the way,' she whispered.

CHAPTER TWENTY-EIGHT

Meanwhile, in Clapham, Myra was entertaining the portly director of a Swiss bank. 'You know, Madame,' he said, as his black moustache glistened with the residue of her best vintage champagne. 'There ees always a place for you on the board. A woman of your charm . . . intelligence . . .'

'Thank you, Monsieur LeFevre. Most kind. I might take you up on that.'

She had always liked Geneva. Geneva was a city that would appreciate her exceptional talents. England had suddenly become so . . . so . . . what was the word? Parochial. Yes. Parochial.

Myra did not know why the forces of the Universe had chosen to repel her, but she was aware that the Coven of Covens would damn her. This did not worry her unduly, for Myra was a Scorpio, ruled by Pluto, dark planet of death, and fixed by water. She knew when it was wise to withdraw from a battle but she was also blessed with the patience required to wait until the time was right to exert her revenge. . . .

CHAPTER TWENTY-NINE

Having stayed the night in Dorset, Merlin and Sheenah drove back to London in Merlin's 1973 Triumph Stag. He dropped her on the corner because he was late for a dream workshop.

'Thanks for everything.' She kissed him lightly on the cheek.

'That's all right.'

Weighed down by the triple-pointed crown and *The Very Moste Secrete Booke of Witchery* encased in a Sainsbury's carrier bag, Sheenah padded slowly down the street. The sun shone warmly on her hair and enhanced a mood already elevated by the promise of adventure. As she drew near her house she perceived, through the tinted lenses of the Paloma Picasso sunglasses, that there was a man standing on her doorstep. A brown man in a brown suit juggling what appeared to be six brown balls.

Astonished, she removed the Palomas and squinted at the figure. The suit was, indeed, brown, the balls were oranges, and the man was Harold.

She grabbed a neighbour's gate for support.

It was Harold.

Deep in concentration, he had not seen her.

The aerial formation of citrus projectiles changed to two by twos.

No wonder.

She had made a wish on the full moon of the night of her coronation, the most magically potent night of her fifty-six-year-long life. No wonder. She should have known better and wished for something sensible – wisdom, perhaps, or a new car. But no. She had gone and wished for Harold.

And here he was.

She walked with shivering knees to her front door.

Harold turned around.

One of the oranges dropped to the ground with a thud.

He stopped juggling and pushed the oranges into his trouser pockets where they created an unseemly bulge.

'Hullo,' he said.

She looked down at him. She had forgotten he was that much smaller. Somehow, over the years, in her mind he had grown tall.

'What are you doing here?'

He seemed embarrassed. 'I was in the neighbourhood, and . . .'

'Where have you been all these years? Everybody thought you were dead.'

'It's a long story. I went back to the circus for a bit and now I'm in showbusiness.'

'Showbusiness?'

'Well. Kind of. I entertain at children's parties. The Great Haroldo. That's why I was practising with these.'

He indicated the fruit in his pockets.

'The Great Haroldo.'

'Yes. It's quite decent money, actually.'

'I'm glad.'

His black eyes gazed into hers. 'What about you?'

'I've just been crowned Queen of the Witches.'

'Oh, my goodness!'

He showed a row of small, even teeth that, if memory served her correctly, were his own. 'How absolutely wonderful!'

Sheenah knew that (apart from Merlin) Harold was the only man in the United Kingdom capable of genuinely appreciating the importance of her achievement and the honour of her appointment.

His face had become shiny with pleasure and he continued smiling broadly.

She felt weak.

'Can I come in, then?' he said.

Sheenah put the key into the lock.

'I suppose you had better,' she replied. 'You've got quite a lot to catch up on.'

the end

185